Nick Yapp
A DOG'S LIFE

Imprimata

Published by **Imprimata**

A CIP Catalogue record for this book is available
from the British Library

ISBN 978-1-906192-63-1

Artwork by Ruby Lescott
Ben's portrait by Maureen Lescott

Designed and typeset by Mark Bracey
Set in Warnock Pro (InDCS5)

Printed in Great Britain

Imprimata

Imprimata Publishers Limited
73 Banstead Road, Ewell, Surrey, KT17 3HH, UK.

To Ruby, for everything...

Nick Yapp has published over 50 books: on cricket, poetry, hoaxers, 20th century history, 'difficult' children, and Hollywood Heroes. *A Dog's Life* is his fourth children's novel, and is the first part of a trilogy.

INTRODUCTION

The tyres hissed and bumped on the wet road as the vehicle sped up the valley into the Green Desert of Wales. Thanks to power steering, the driver needed only one hand on the wheel to guide the vehicle through the twists and turns of a road that skirted boulders, clung to the high ground where it crossed the marshy plateau, and stroked its way round the massive curves of the mountains themselves. The rain didn't bother him. He knew this road well. Though he was driving with only sidelights that barely lit the road for more than a metre or two, he made good speed.

There were other vehicles on the road, other drivers taking care not to draw attention to themselves, though only the Devil knew who'd be on the lookout for anything odd in this wilderness, at this hour.

'Bit of a crowd tonight,' said the driver.

His mate, sitting beside him, laughed. 'It's a growing sport.'

'But you don't get this on TV Saturday afternoon, do you,' said the driver. 'Not even on Sky Sports.'

'That'll be the day.'

The driver muttered a curse at a sheep that had wandered into the road. 'You packed everything?' he asked.

'Everything. Netting...buckets and sponges'

'Sawdust?'

'Sawdust...first-aid box...After all, we don't want any *unnecessary* suffering, do we?' They both laughed.

'Lanterns?'

'...and the scales. And the shotties.'

They laughed again.

'Gotta have the shotties. And we've got the contestants nice and cosy in their crates.'

'Ready and waiting. Warm-ups and main attractions.' The driver changed gear as they came to a steep bend, then accelerated along a rare straight stretch of road. They were in a hurry to reach the destination and set up the arena. It would be a long and busy night – with risks attached. But, if all went as planned, there'd be plenty of cash to take home in the early hours of the morning – a fair exchange for a corpse or two dropped down a disused mineshaft...

CHAPTER 1

Two eggs, two sausages, two thick rashers, tomato, bread and dip. These fry-ups would kill him in the end, that and his precious "smokes", but Gwynedd wasn't going to argue with him about his tea, not when it was Friday night and she desperately needed to cadge a bit of money off him.

'You got any cash, Gran...' Bloody hell, she'd nearly called him "Grandad". Hadn't done that for years. All that rubbish had finished years ago, when he had told her that her mum and dad had always called him "Dave", and she had decided to do the same. It was a kind of link with her parents – about the only one she had. 'You got any cash, Dave?'

No answer. That's it, miserable old git. He's pretending not to hear, stupid old fool. 'You want more baccy and ciggie papers tonight, you'll have to give me some money!!' He'll have heard that. There's no way he can pretend he hasn't.

'What you done with all the money I give you yesterday?'

Lying old git. He didn't hand over no money yesterday – nor the day before, come to think. She banged the cooker with the knife she was using to turn the sausages and bacon, sending a spray of hot fat up the kitchen wall.

'Wiped my bum with it. What d'you think?'

She flipped the rashers over. Dave was fussy about his bacon. If she fried it till it was dark and crackly, he threw it out of the window, with some smart remark about how it would be more use keeping the slugs off his lettuces. If she didn't fry it enough, he complained that, if he'd wanted live pig, he'd have gone to Rhayader market. She broke the two eggs into the large pan, black and crinkled with age. Gwynedd could remember her ma using the same pan on the same hob on the same old electric cooker. That was before ma and dad disappeared, before they 'pissed off', as Dave so charmingly put it. Bastards. There had been no warning, no note, no explanation, no forwarding address – just a card every Christmas, and, if she was lucky, a card for her birthday - usually a few days late.

She tilted the pan to make it easier to splash fat over the eggs, and cook them on both sides, the way Dave liked them. God alone knew how many eggs she'd cooked for his teas over the years since ma and dad left. How long now? Years and years and years, girl. You was only little when you started, standing on a box to reach over the cooker. And it's gone on and on, every day since.

The eggs bubbled into a quick cooked froth, flecked

with chips of burnt salt off the cheap bacon. She switched off the hob, and allowed herself a bit of fun arranging the food on a plate. She made the sausages into a big fat mouth, with the eggs as eyes, and the dip as though it was snot coming from a tomato nose. She took one rasher of bacon and fixed it like a tongue coming out of the sausage mouth. She couldn't be bothered to think what to do with the other rasher, so she shoved it under the bread, on the edge of the plate, and took it all through to the front room. There was not a word of thanks from Dave, let alone bloody artistic appreciation.

'Where's the rest of the bacon,' he said. 'What's wrong with it?'

She pushed the fried bread aside, revealing the second rasher. 'Money,' she said, and held out her hand.

'I give you money this morning.'

'Three days ago,' said Gwynedd. 'And it wouldn't kill you to say "thank you, Gwynedd" once in a million years.' Waste of breath, really. He never called her by her name.

'That's the deal, though, isn't it,' he said. 'You look after me and I look after you. It's good enough for me, and it's good enough for Social Services, so whether it's good or not for you don't enter into it.' He slashed a sausage in two and bunged one half in his mouth.

He's right, girl. It is the deal. Without Dave you'd be in care, fostered with some poncey do-gooders, or in a home, some God forsaken institution, anywhere within a twenty mile radius. Instead of which, here you are, in a comfy bungalow, smack in the middle of Wales, and scarce fifteen minutes from town. You reckon life's bad? It could be a lot worse. Yeah, but this is Friday night. No school tomorrow. Life *should* be a lot better than this, but that would take money.

'Come on, Dave,' she said. 'I got to have money.'

'You'll get some in the morning. Now, let a man eat in peace.'

Gwynedd went back into the kitchen, tipped the hot fat back into the dripping bowl, and opened the window to throw out the bacon rind for the birds. It had stopped raining, and the wind was blowing the clouds away. The air outside smelt fresh and clean, better than the stale tobacco and the ancient damp inside. She fancied a walk, down to the chippie. That young Paki lad behind the counter might give her a bag of chips on credit. She could make him laugh easily enough, and he always gave her a good looking-over with his big brown eyes - at least as big and as brown as hers - whenever she went in. She recognised the look. You could see that in Rhayader market, when the farmers were checking out the breeding stock.

She tidied the kitchen and went back to the front room. Dave had finished his tea – it never took long. 'You got a mouth like the Severn Tunnel,' she said. He was flicking through the channels on the telly, and took no notice.

'You swear you got no money?'

He waved her away. She went into the bathroom, and washed her hands carefully, to get rid of the stink of cooking. Then she sat at the little table in her bedroom and tarted herself up. Often she didn't like her looks, but tonight she was generous in her judgement on the face in the mirror. It was all right. The eyes were good. The hair was OK, black and glossy. The bones were good. The mouth looked like what they call "sensual", not like it did on bad days, when it looked like the two fat sausages she'd just cooked. Great, she reckoned. Here she was, Friday night and the whole weekend ahead, with no blooming school till Monday. A bit of make-up, and maybe the earrings, and that Paki lad would be only too happy to slip her a bag of chips – salt and vinegar and all.

'I'm going out.'

Dave's grunt registered neither approval nor disapproval. She stood in the front room doorway and looked at the back of his head. There were far more grey hairs than black now. Not that he was truly ancient – only recently qualified for his Old Age Pension – but he behaved old when it suited. And it suited most of the time.

He clicked the sound down on the telly. 'Got your mobile?' he said.

How stupid can you get? 'What's the point? You got no phone here. I can't call you, and you can't call me.'

'In case you need the police,' he said.

Well, bless us. There's a pathetic attempt to suggest that he's looking after me. Goes straight to the heart, doesn't it. No way. Makes you feel like puking. But it don't make no odds anyway, because there ain't no credit on the bloody mobile.

She slipped the front door key into the pocket of her red jeans, made sure that her sweater was pulled down immaculate like, and set off down the lane, heading for town. It was the way she always went – the way that led to the shops, the school bus, her mates, and fish and chips. She couldn't remember when she had last gone the other way, up into the old mountains. Not for years. No point. There were some that simply wouldn't go up there. Little Huwie swore blind there were banshees, with eyes like car headlights... not that he had the least idea what a banshee was. There were others that talked about "strange goings on" in the old hills, but Gwynedd didn't believe a word of that. No, she didn't go up there because there simply wasn't any point.

It was a bright, clear, golden evening, warm by late May standards, and the birds were singing away as though they were paid to. She clattered along the tarmac road, in a pair of shoes that she'd bought off Lynn at school. They were too big for her, so they kept slipping and the heels hit the road before her feet were ready to, but that didn't matter, they was good shoes. She was swinging her hips and her earrings, and she felt great. Going out was the right thing to do. She decided she would call in at Sam's cottage on the way to the chippie, to show him what a catch he could have in her. What a beauty. Better than that, she would boss him into coming to the chippie with her. Double prize for that: one, Sam's mum would give him money for fish and chips, and two, she could play one lad off against the other. That'd be fun - wake the Paki lad up a bit, and hopefully open Sam's lovely eyes to what a gorgeous young lady he had with him.

She liked Sam. He wasn't like the other lads. Not hoping for a groping all the time, quite the opposite. Backward in coming forward, that was Sam. But he made her laugh. He was like a brother, which was handy, because she had no brother and Sam had no sister. Better than a brother, he was a mate... had been since Juniors.

She and Sam had a good routine going. Every morning they met in the field down by the river, then walked together to the car park to catch the school bus. Every afternoon, they left the school bus and walked home together – Sam to his cottage and his mum, Gwynedd to her bungalow and bloody Dave. Just good mates, nothing romantic, though there was no harm in making that cow Mollie think there might be.

Gwynedd checked her clattering stride. She realised she was charging down the lane as though she was in a desperate hurry or someone was chasing her. She put her hand over her mouth. Oh my God, if the girls in the gang saw her rushing full tilt to Sam Harper's cottage they'd give her a bad time for a whole week.

As she neared the cottage, Gwynedd flicked off her shoes. Always worthwhile taking people by surprise. You learned a lot that way. The cottage was separated from the road by the narrowest of gardens. There was a scrappy hedge of bramble, hazel and hawthorn, and a couple of paving slabs that served as a short path, and there you were – at the white-painted front door. Or rather, at the front window, peering in. The lights were on. Becky and Sam were at home, as usual.

As she craned her neck to get a better look, one of her earrings smacked against the glass. Shit! Silly clumsy bitch! She saw Sam and his mother look up suddenly. They were sitting on the sofa with some book. Sam saw her and leapt off the sofa like someone had shoved a stag-beetle up his arse. He put his face against the glass and stuck his tongue out at her. She stuck hers out at him.

'Let us in, Sam,' she shouted, and slipped her heels back on.

It was nice in what Sam and Becky called the "sitting-room" and Gwynedd called the "front room". Log fire going, bright rug on the floor, lots of cushions everywhere. There was a couple of glasses out, too. Sam was drinking coke, but that looked more like ginger wine in Becky's glass. She'd started early, and, as always, she was all smiles. If Becky come home and found a burglar, she'd be all smiles. Dead opposite of Dave.

'Would you like something to drink, Gwynedd?'

'I'll have a ginger wine, thanks, Mrs Harper.'

'I don't think we've got any ginger wine,' said Becky.

'What's that, then?' Gwynedd pointed at the glass.

'That's sherry,' said Sam.

'Glass of sherry'll do nicely.' Gwynedd knew there was no way Becky would give her alcohol, but there was no harm in making people feel awkward.

'Don't be daft. I'll get you a coke.' Sam went into the kitchen.

'What you been looking at?' Gwynedd took Sam's place next to Becky on the sofa.

'Old photographs.'

'I love old photos. You got any of little Sam, naked, on a rug?' She flicked a couple of pages. 'Who's that?'

'That's Steve. Sam's father. It's the last photo I ever took of him. He became ill after that.' Becky took a sip of her sherry.

'He don't look ill,' said Gwynedd.

'No. It all happened very quickly.'

Gwynedd sensed sympathy was required of her. 'Ah,' she said. 'Do you miss him? Bet you do.'

'We both do.'

Sam returned with Gwynedd's coke.

'Looking at pictures of your dad,' she said.

He put the drink down and took the photo album from her hands. 'Probably seen enough of that tonight.'

There was a bang on the door. It was the Paki lad from the chippie. Becky had ordered a home delivery of fish and chips.

Becky fiddled with her purse. 'I'm afraid we only ordered for two.'

'How about a miracle, then?' said Gwynedd. 'Divide it up like they do in the Bible?' She looked at them. No, nothing doing there. Best get out the way. 'Hang on,' she said to the Paki lad. 'You can give us a ride into town on your scooter.'

'What about your drink?' said Sam.

'Put it back in the can. I'll take it with me.'

'It came out of a bottle.'

'Put it back in the bottle, then.'

'It's a two litre bottle.'

'That's very kind of you,' said Gwynedd. 'Make sure you screw the cap back on tight. Don't want to spoil my clothes. I'll call for you in the morning, Sam. Night, Becky.'

Three minutes later, Gwynedd was clutching her bottle of coke in the warmth of the chippie. The Paki lad gave her a bag of chips with his long slender hands, and a good going-over with his smashing eyes.

As she munched and walked slowly back up the hill to the bungalow, she thought about Sam and Becky. Sam got no man in his life, and I got no woman in mine. Pity that Dave and Becky didn't fancy each other, didn't want to get together... but then Becky would have to be mad to fancy a bloke like Dave.

And what does she think about you, girl? Not good enough for her Sam, most likely. You don't know that. She's always friendly enough. But would that last if she knew you fancied him? She wouldn't want you for a daughter-in-law. Don't be daft, we ain't talking about that. But that's the only way you'd ever get her as your ma. I don't want her as a ma. I got a ma. Yeah, somewhere. Anyway, that's enough of that sort of thinking. Silly to make yourself miserable. Think of something else. Maybe that Paki lad peered through the Harper's window before he knocked on the door.

Maybe he'd seen her with Sam. Maybe that's why he give you the chips. Maybe your little scheme to play off one lad against another come off, after all. Hope so. You got to keep on hoping and planning in life, otherwise, what's the point?

CHAPTER 2

As she had promised, Gwynedd called for Sam next morning – not just because you *had* to keep your word to a mate, but also because mates didn't come any better than Sam. But every time you do a good deed you get a needle stuck in your bum, and she had the dubious pleasure of Dave's company when she set off.

'Can't you shuffle faster than this?'

'Not if I don't want to,' he said.

'It'll be Monday morning by the time we get there.'

It was a matter of stubborn pride with Dave always to grace the Post Office with his presence to collect his old age pension. Time and again she'd offered to do it for him, but he said he didn't trust her with his money.

'Why don't you get it on a Thursday, like all the other senile citizens?'

'Damn cheek!' He aimed a blow at her leg with his stick. 'I don't need the money on Thursday. I can wait. I ain't like the others.'

'Didn't have enough money last night, did you,' said

Gwynedd. 'And what you wearing a suit for? It's your pension you're picking up, not a bloody medal from the Queen.'

He aimed another blow at her. She stepped nimbly aside. 'Got out of bed the wrong side did you?' he said. 'As per bloody usual.'

'Shut your mouth!' He was right, though. She was in a bad mood, pissed off because she hadn't had the money to top up her mobile, so it was still out of action. It was a lousy mobile anyway, as that cow Mollie had pointed out the day they met. It had been loathing at first sight. When Mollie Pryce had come to town the winter before last, Gwynedd had looked at her as a potential ally in the fight against almost everyone and everything. Here was someone with guts enough to tell the world where to go, someone who kept her head well out of books and all that rubbish. What changed all that was the speed with which Mollie stole all Gwynedd's mates. Gwynedd hadn't seen what was happening until it was done and the cold wind of loneliness hit her. She had her first fight with Mollie, which resulted in a draw and a three-day suspension for Gwynedd. Mollie, then a new pupil at the school got off with a caution, and used those three days to strengthen her hold on her "gang", as she called them. On her return to school, Gwynedd spent another three days wondering how Mollie had done it. There were no signs of bribery or bullying being employed. When she quizzed her former mates, they laughed nervously and said Mollie was "great".

Gwynedd now hated everything about Mollie. She hated the way she dressed – all flash and bling-bling. She hated the way Mollie sneered at everything local. She hated the way Mollie hinted at a richer, smarter, faster social life. Gwynedd hated not knowing if this was true, or just talk. Silly to get so worked up, when it was likely a tissue of lies. The point was, nobody knew much about Mollie, who never let anyone into her life out of school, save for when she hung around town after school, or when she was flashing her money around at the caff on Saturday mornings. So there was no need for Sam to go on about confining her war with Mollie to school hours and school premises. What else could she do? She still didn't know where Mollie lived, didn't even know whether she had a mum and dad, brothers or sisters. Mollie didn't tell, and Gwynedd wasn't going to ask. She didn't want Mollie to get the idea that she was the slightest bit interested in the cow.

Dave's parting shot, as he left her at Sam's cottage, was 'Behave yourself.'

'Don't be so bloody cheeky,' said Gwynedd. 'Just make sure you get money for the housekeeping. And some for me.'

'You want money, you get a Saturday job. You're old enough.'

'I already got a seven-days-a-week job looking after you.' No one got the last word with Gwynedd, thanks very much.

Boosted by this petty exchange, she banged on

the cottage door. There was a burst of barking - that bloomin' dog - then the door opened, and there was Sam with a face like sour milk.

'Hallo, Sam darling. Where's that smile?'

He drew his mouth into a mirthless leer.

'Bloody rotten smile, that is. How about a razzle-dazzle smile?'

'You wait till you hear what's going on.'

They went into the kitchen. Becky was sitting at the table, with a letter in her hands. She smiled up at Gwynedd. 'Hallo,' she said. 'I've just had a letter.'

Well, that's bleeding obvious for a start, girl. And, from the thunderous look on Sam's face when he opened the door, this letter obviously ain't brought good news as far as he's concerned. So this is no time for bright, chirpy remarks. Best get whatever it is out into the open, get it over.

'Has someone died?' she said.

'No. It's good news,' said Becky. 'At least, *I* think it is. I've been offered a job...'

Sam interrupted her. 'In Bristol,' he said. 'You know, Bristol. I mean... Bristol!'

'What sort of job?'

'Working in a Retirement Home. As Deputy Supervisor.' Gwynedd noted the pride in Becky's voice. 'I haven't got it yet, mind you.' Becky looked anxiously at Sam. 'I'll have to go for an interview, but Martin – the person that wrote this letter – thinks that will be a mere formality.'

Right, thought Gwynedd, so there's this bloke Martin

that fancies you and wants to lure you to Bristol. No wonder darling Sam looks as though he's just gargled with vinegar.

'You going to accept?' Gwynedd tapped her foot on the floor. Come on, Becky, just give us a quick answer, yes or no. We don't need to hear all about the money you got from the insurance when Sam's dad died seven years ago, and how it's nearly all gone. Heard that one often enough, ta very much. That's tough, but it ain't special. We've all got money problems, though they're not really problems for the likes of you, because somehow you can buy your way out of them.

'Bristol's a lovely city,' said Becky, 'and there's a flat that goes with the job. Of course, it's very beautiful here, but it's getting more and more difficult to keep the cottage going, with the maintenance and the bills.'

'Everyone gets bills.' Gwynedd glanced at Sam, and then back at Becky.

She's not listening to you, girl. She wants to talk about Bristol, and the shops and the schools, the art galleries and the theatres, the harbour, the trains, the buses, the drainage... Bristol gutters most likely got the best litter in the world, from the sound of it. Bet even the spit on the pavements is top class. Time to put a stop to all this.

'Sam's got a good enough school here.'

'But, Gwynedd, you're always saying your school's awful.'

'That's a lie. I never said it was "awful". That's not one of my words. I just said it was crap and a dump and I'd like to torch the place. Anyway, it don't matter what I think. Sam likes it.'

'So he's been trying to convince me,' said Becky. 'But I keep explaining to him – we can't stay here. We have to do something. I have to get some money, and that means a job. And a job with a flat means we can sell this place.'

The silly thing was that neither of them looked one million per cent keen on the idea. Sam don't want to go. Becky knows he don't want to go. It's like me and Dave – both of us angry and miserable because the other one's angry and miserable. Bit of a difference, though. Becky and Sam like each other. Must be strange, living with someone you're truly fond of.

'Come on, Sam,' she said. 'Let's go up the town.'

Dave would be knocking back his pension in the nearest pub by now. Time to pay him a visit, get some money off him, and take Sam to the caff to cheer him up.

'I'd be a mug not to accept this offer,' said Becky.

Gwynedd turned to Sam. 'There you are,' she said. 'Your mum's made her mind up. She wants the pair of you out of this place, and there's no more to be said. So let's get that razzle-dazzle smile back on your lovely face before the wind changes and you get stuck with your Mister Grumps face for life.' Total waste of breath. Neither of them was interested in what she was saying.

Becky gave a nervous laugh. There wasn't a flicker from Sam.

'Oh, come on, Harper,' said Gwynedd. 'Give us a smile like you used to give Mrs Hamilton, when she caught you not paying attention in class.'

'When was that?' said Becky.

'Sixth of May, three years ago,' said Sam. 'Quarter past two in the afternoon. OK, Gwynedd. Let's go.'

That's more like it.

Ten minutes later Gwynedd and Sam left Dave moaning into his pint of bitter, and headed for *La Strada*, the all-purpose eaterie that catered for everyone. Gwynedd loved it – the bright strip lights, the noise bouncing off the Formica-topped tables and tiled floor, the warmth, and the big windows that allowed a perfect view if anything ever happened in the street outside.

They sat facing each other, drinking cans of coke.

'Come on, then. What's wrong with Bristol?'

He made a noise like a fart. 'You fancy living in a Retirement Home?'

'Nice,' she said. 'Quiet.'

'Old people smell.'

'So do you.'

'They let food dribble out of the corners of their mouths.'

'So do you.'

'They piss themselves.'

'So do you.'

'I don't.'

'You did. When we had that supply teacher in Year 3.'

'Never!'

'You did.'

'I don't make a habit of it.'

'Stand up and show us your crotch now.'

He did as he was told. She snatched up her can of coke, leaned forward and sloshed it on his lap. 'There you are. You got wet trousers.'

'Bitch!'

'Misery! God, I wouldn't like to have to live with you.'

It wasn't exactly true. She'd been thinking about it last night, lying in bed and wondering what life would be like if she and Dave and Sam and Becky all lived together. Well, maybe not Dave. They could put him in a home. Serve him right. He'd threatened to do that to her often enough. So... just Sam and me and Becky. Life would be busy, noisy, lovely. But now, sitting in *La Strada*, Gwynedd came to the same conclusion she'd reached last night. There was no way it was going to happen. Even more so this morning, with Becky so keen to take Sam off to Bristol. Best swallow that down your throat quick, like popping pills.

'Anyway,' she said, 'your mum didn't say you was going to live in this Retirement Home. She said there'd be a flat with the job. That's where you'll live. Not with the old loonies.'

'There'll be the stink of disinfectant.'

'And farts.'

'And loads of mucus,' he said.

'What's mucus?'

'It's what drips out of your nose.'

'No, that's snot.'

'It's real name is mucus.'

She hated it when he used posh words. 'Drink your

blooming coke,' she said. 'Like I say, you won't be living with the loonies.'

'I know. And of course I'll go to Bristol, for mum's sake. But I'll miss you...' His voice trailed off.

She suddenly felt very uncomfortable, like she'd sat on a wasp. It was time to change the subject, quick. 'Don't be so bloody soft,' she said. 'Tell me about this Martin. The bloke that wrote your mum the letter. He fancies her, doesn't he.'

'I don't know.'

'Course he does. Does she fancy him?'

'How should I know?'

'What's he like? Have you ever met him?'

'Might have done. Yes. He used to hang around, after dad died. I think he'd known mum before. He was the guy who drove us to the cottage, when we first came here. He brought us and mum's special belongings when we moved. He used to phone mum.'

'How often?'

'I don't know!'

'No,' she said. 'You don't know anything unless it's on the blooming Internet. But did he phone her, like, every night or once a week or what?' She took a deep breath and spoke nicely, in a voice that couldn't possibly give offence. 'Are they having an affair?' She meant it as a compliment. 'Becky's an attractive woman. That's where you get your good looks, my lovely Sam. Stands to reason blokes would fancy her. And if this Martin was offering her a job, only natural he'd want something in return.'

'Let's change the subject.'

'I don't want to change the bloody subject.' Her mind kept coming back to Sam's words, that he would miss her.

'Would you really miss me?' She stretched out her hand to take his.

'It's not just you. The real problem's Ben.'

She withdrew her hand.

'That bloody dog! You use it like a weapon. If you don't want to do anything, you say it's cos you've got to take Ben for a walk. If you're bored and can't wait to slip away, you say it's 'cos you've got to feed Ben. Always Ben! Ben, Ben, bloody Ben... What's the matter? Seen a ghost?'

Sam was staring over her shoulder. His face had gone beetroot red. She looked round, and there was Mollie the Cow Pryce right behind her, with a dirty grin on her face.

'How long you bin snoopin' on a private conversation?' said Gwynedd.

'You don't snoop on conversations. You eavesdrop,' said Mollie. 'And, if you ask me, that wasn't a conversation. It was a row.'

'Yeah? Well, I don't hear anyone asking you!'

Sam was not a fan of friction. 'I'm moving to Bristol,' he said.

'Glad to be rid of you,' muttered Gwynedd.

Mollie slipped into the chair beside Sam. 'Oh, Sam,' she said. 'What a shame. You'll lose touch with all your mates, all of us that's so very fond of you. Especially me. What'll I do without you?' She gazed at him and fluttered her eyelashes.

Gwynedd wished she had some coke left in her can. Mollie could do with a wash.

Mollie held her gaze on Sam. 'And what about *poor* Ben?'

'That dog don't matter a fag end to you. So don't pretend!'

'I dunno what to do with Ben,' said Sam.

'Have him put down.' As soon as the words were out of her mouth, Gwynedd wished she hadn't said them. Sam gave her the sourest look she'd ever seen, and Mollie took his hand.

'Oh, Sam,' she said. 'Isn't that a dreadful thing for anyone to say.'

Gwynedd stormed out of the café and began running towards the crossroads in the centre of town. She really hadn't meant to say that. She liked Ben… a bit. And it would be horrible if Sam went to Bristol. She wanted to put things right. Immediately. A text! That was what texts were for. Her mind quickly composed the message: DRST SAM DNT MEAN THT BOUT BEN SRY PLS CN WE MT SNASPOS? G XX. No, she'd make that XXXXXX, to prove how sorry she was. She got as far as pulling her mobile out of her pocket before she remembered she hadn't topped it up.

And there was the bloody clock tower at the bloody crossroads, saying it was half past twelve – time to get Dave's dinner. She wiped the tears quickly from her eyes, and forced herself to do the shopping. She bought a couple of chops and some more bangers, eggs, tins of beans and a bit of cheese. There'd be potatoes and stuff out of the garden at the bungalow, but she grabbed a couple of loaves to see the two of them through the weekend. Then she stamped her way back home, her sorrow already replaced by anger. Good luck to Sam and Mollie, she thought. See how he likes spending the afternoon with that dirty scumbag.

Back at the bungalow, she bunged the three biggest spuds they had in the microwave and started frying the chops and a couple of bangers. Dave hated things grilled. She kept telling him fried food would clog up his blood, but he reckoned grilled meat had no juice in it. People are so stupid, always doing what's bad for them. She just wanted to smash them when they were like that.

As she cooked, she tried to pull herself together, to take stock of the situation. Sam was going to Bristol. There was nothing she could do about that. She didn't want him to go, but he was going. And he was worried about Ben. She'd help him. He was a mate. She'd help Sam find a home for Ben. Maybe... maybe Ben could move in with her and Dave? Ben was OK, a good dog in some ways. The microwave pinged. She prodded the spuds and decided to give them another couple of minutes. For one thing, Ben didn't go after sheep. That mattered. A dog that chased sheep didn't last long in mid-Wales. Ask any farmer. It's out with the shotgun and out with the dog's brains if they chase sheep. Not a nice thought when you're doing the cooking...

Dave came home on the dot of one, as usual, wiping his mouth and belching loudly. Gwynedd didn't say anything about Sam, or about Ben. She had decided she'd give Dave his dinner first, then bring up the subject, kind of diplomatic like. He complained about the baked potatoes, telling her for the hundredth time that the skins never crisp up in the microwave, though it didn't stop him wolfing them down with everything else, including half the fat from the frying pan. She was just about to mention Ben when there was a knock at the door.

It was Skinny Vinnie, the Last Lad You'd Want To See.

'Hallo, Gwynedd,' he said. 'It's me, Vinnie.'

She stood in the doorway, barring his way. There were those at school that reckoned Vinnie fancied her, and maybe he did. He'd tried it on a couple of times, but she'd made it clear he wasn't getting anywhere, and he'd never pushed it. He was a strange lad – tall and stringy, with a face that flirted with acne without ever succumbing to it. He was a loner, a bit of a nerd. Well, that's what happens to people when their parents are too pushy and want them to get 1000 Grade As in the bloomin' exams that loomed ever closer. Gwynedd had already decided she'd take a term off when they came round in a couple of years' time.

'You gonna let us in?'

Gwynedd led Vinnie to the kitchen, telling him he could stay just as long as it took him to do the washing up, and that she'd go for a walk with him later if he did. She had her fingers crossed at the time, so felt no guilt when she kicked Vinnie out of the bungalow half an hour later. She went back to the kitchen, knowing that she'd have to re-do the washing up. Vinnie had left smears of fat on all the plates, and bits of food on the knives and forks. There was still old sugar encrusted on the bottoms of all the tea mugs.

When she gave Dave his tea later, she asked him about having Ben to live with them in the bungalow. He didn't go up the wall. He just calmly said 'not bloody ever', and turned up the sound on the telly so that it was impossible to argue.

Later, she remembered just in time to run into town to top up her mobile. It was the only good thing that had happened all day.

CHAPTER 3

Gwynedd woke early on Monday morning, glad that the weekend was over. The scene in the caff was preying on her mind. She'd been a fool to walk out of there and leave Sam all alone with Mollie. The cow would have fastened her claws into him good and proper, and forced poor Sam to make promises he's been regretting ever since. Gwynedd cursed her own stupidity. She shouldn't have lost it with Sam and Mollie. What she should have done was sit on her bloody pride and called to see him yesterday, to get all this sorted before the start of another week of school. It was too late now, she told herself. Monday had come round and she hadn't been to see him and she had to live with that and get up and get on with what had to be done.

She went on cursing herself as she washed, put on her school clothes, and went into the kitchen to make Dave's early morning cuppa. She wondered if Sam's weekend had been any better than her own. He'd had Becky to look after him, of course, and that stupid dog for company. Who needed dogs? Dolls were better than dogs any day. She'd had a word with her own Sasha yesterday. Taken her out and played with her. Dressed her up, told her a few secrets, and then slammed her back in the box with all the other Trash 'n Treasure because the silly doll had made her cry. You couldn't do that with a dog.

'Where's my bloody tea?'

Gwynedd let the teabag stew in the boiling water, and then took the mug and plonked it on the floor outside Dave's room. She banged on the door. 'Your tea's where it is every bloody morning,' she shouted, and returned to the kitchen to make his breakfast.

She'd leapt out of bed this morning, determined to get back in control of her life. But that feeling had soon gone. She was dragging her heels, deliberately running the risk of leaving too little time to call for Sam. Only when she had given Dave his bacon and beans did she see the foolishness of what she was doing.

You got to see Sam sooner or later, she told herself. So you might as well get it over, right? Right! But I don't want to go and knock for him.

She grabbed her bag and raced from the bungalow, avoiding the lane that led to the Sam's cottage and taking the path across the fields, down to the trees that fringed the river Wye. She sprinted over the footbridge and into the Kid's Playground, half-hoping that she'd find him there, half-hoping she wouldn't. The playground was empty. Maybe he'd arranged to meet Mollie. She chucked her bag on to the grass, and climbed the chains of one of the swings, until she could haul herself up on to the crossbar. Time passed more quickly if you kept yourself busy, so she flung herself into a series of gymnastic exercises while she waited. She was good at gymnastics. She'd proved it over and over in the happier, daredevil days of Bryn Mawr Juniors, to poor old Mr Richards and poor old Mrs Hamilton as they'd stood below and exhausted their respective threats and bribes to try to get her to come down from netball hoops, wall-bars, goalposts.

And then Sam appeared. The moment she saw him, she leapt to the ground. The huge grin on her face was immediate, wide and genuine. She rushed up to him. 'So... you going to Bristol?'

He nodded. 'Mum says she's putting the cottage on the market today.'

'I'll miss you, Sam,' she said. They sat very still together on adjacent swings. Then she slipped her hand into his and gave it a gentle squeeze.

Very softly, he said 'Ow.'

They were spared the embarrassment of not knowing what to do next by the clatter of feet over the footbridge and the arrival of Little Huwie at full pelt.

'Two minutes to the bus... and counting!' he shouted.

The three of them ran through the campsite that bordered the little park, crossed the main road with more speed than sense, and dashed into the car park. The school bus was pulling away, but the driver drew up and waited for them. As they boarded the bus, Mollie called out to Sam.

'Here, Sammy. You comin' to keep your promise? I got a hot seat waitin' for you.'

'Shut yer face. He's with me now.' Gwynedd bundled Sam into a window seat and positioned herself between him and Mollie.

'You shut your's. He bloody promised,' said Mollie.

So she was after a row, was she? That was more like it. 'Yeah, well, he's bloody breaking his bloody promise,' said Gwynedd. 'You can have sexy Huwie instead.'

With a shove from Gwynedd, Little Huwie fell into the seat next to Mollie. He did what he could to protect himself as Gwynedd and Mollie traded insults and punches across his body. The driver threatened to stop the bus, but he'd made that threat too often in the past for anyone to take any notice. By the time they reached Llandrindod Wells, Little Huwie was on the verge of tears and Gwynedd was ready for a full-scale fight. Sam nipped smartly off the bus, and with studied politeness thanked the driver for the ride.

'One of these days...' The driver shook his head.

It started to rain. Mollie and Gwynedd carried their row into school and made it last through History, Maths, a double English lesson on *Wizards* ('...compare and contrast Gandalf, Harry Potter, Merlin and Derren Browne.' 'Miss, who's Derren Browne?' 'Just get on with your work...'), and most of the dinner break. Not until they each had a bag of hot chips in their grasp and a separate group of friends in tow did they leave one other alone. In the afternoon, the rain stopped and after what seemed like months to Gwynedd, the school day ended. Sam dodged Mollie's outstretched arms, but she caught him with her foot and he fell up the steps into the bus, where Gwynedd hauled him to the safety of the back seat. Forty rowdy minutes later, she and Sam were back in the campsite.

Gwynedd took off her shoes, rolled up the legs of her trousers, and sat on a small rock by the river. She dipped her feet in the swirling waters. Sam sat behind and above her, on a large boulder. They had their backs to the half dozen tents of early season campers. Since junior school days, this was where they had always discussed the events of the day, the state of the world, all their hopes, dreams and troubles.

'And you've told your ma you don't want to go?'

'Yep.'

'And she says you've gotta go?'

'Yep.'

'Then you've gotta go.'

'And that's it?' said Sam. 'That's the result of more than 48 hours brain-storming on your part?'

'What about your brain-storming, then?'

'I don't storm my brain. I nurse it.'

'Is it sick?'

'I nurse it because it's a highly delicate instrument. Look at the way it's picked up your bloody Welsh grammar!'

'Don't be so blessed English,' she said. 'That's the language of my forefathers you're talking about.'

'Four fathers, my bum,' he said. 'We haven't got one between us.'

She came to sit next to him on the boulder.

'I don't want you to go any more than you do,' she said. 'I like us being together. I don't want to sit next to anyone else on the bus. If I'm gonna have to walk through here every morning... on my own... well, I'll miss you.' She felt awkward. This was soppy talk. 'I'll miss your deliriously happy face,' she said. 'No, I'm kidding. I know you're not happy. But we have to make the best of life, don't we. It'll be as bad for Ben as it is for you, but he'll have to make a go of it without you. Maybe, wherever they are, my ma and dad are having to make the most of being without me. It's a thought, isn't it?' She began to feel a bit better. She always did when she and Sam talked together. That was the great thing about Sam. You could talk to him about hopes or troubles, didn't matter which, and always end up feeling a bit better than when you started.

'I suppose it really isn't possible for you to have Ben?'

'No way. Dave says he'll never have a dog. Besides, he'd never look after it. Can't look after himself. A dog'd be more bother for me and I've got enough on my plate as it is. Which reminds me, Dave'll be wanting his tea. That's your fault, Sam. I was going straight home and you waylaid me.'

'OK,' he said. 'I'll race you to the bridge.'

She snatched up her bag and sprinted after him. When it came to sheer speed, he could match or beat her most days, but it was always a good contest. Today, after a couple of dozen paces, she stopped running. What's the point, girl? What difference does it make if he wins or you win? There won't be any more races once he's gone to Bristol.

She saw him glance over his shoulder, and stop when he saw that she wasn't racing after him. She trotted up to him and they crossed the footbridge with her arm linked in his. They reached the lane and followed it to Sam's cottage. This was where they parted, every day after school. This was where they always said 'see you tomorrow', and went their separate ways. She tried to kick the thought out of her mind that there was now a limit to the number of times they would be saying such things to each other in the future.

Gwynedd let go of his arm. Best to try to settle into a new regime quickly, like if you was put in prison or taken into hospital. No good going on now as though all was well. Yeah, but maybe Sam will make Becky change her mind, and not go to Bristol. Some bloody hope.

As they reached the cottage, Ben shot round the corner, and greeted them both with a welcome that bordered on madness. The dog clamped his jaws on Sam's bag and tried to drag him into the garden. It was a common welcome home game, but for once Sam made little response. The dog decided what they both needed was a present, and went to fetch one of his favourite stones to share with them.

'Don't worry.' Gwynedd took hold of Sam's hand, remembered how Mollie had done the same thing that morning, and immediately let go of it again. 'I'll think of something. I've got a bigger brain than you... more mature, 'cos I'm older...'

'Three months! That's all.'

'...and I don't have to waste my brain doing foreign languages like Welsh and Algebranese all day and sitting up half the night in some bloomin' internet chat room with Loonie and Wah-Boy and BTM and all the other nerdy losers...' She cut short his protest. 'Yes, you do. And I know you keep it a secret from Becky. It's OK.' She wanted to convince him, for she was trying to summon up great faith in herself. 'Something will turn up. See you tomorrow.' She stood there, looking at him, still holding his hand, while the dog chased round them barking joyfully. It was as though neither of them knew what to do next.

She let go of his hand, turned and ran quickly up the lane and out of sight. With Ben leaping at his heels, Sam shuffled over the two paving slabs and let himself into the cottage.

CHAPTER 4

Something did turn up.

It was July. The cottage had been on the market for five weeks without any sign of a buyer. Every day Gwynedd asked Sam if anyone had come to see it, and every day he said "no", and they gave each other 'high fives'. But they didn't dance for joy, for the threat was always there.

'I just want the thing finished,' said Sam. 'Every day mum cleans the place from top to toilet, and vacuums the garden, and complains about Ben's biscuit crumbs and Ben's slobber and Ben's hairs, as if it's all his fault. And she goes on and on about hoping someone will make an offer for the cottage. No one's even been to see it yet.'

'And what about you?'

'I suffer,' he said. 'I am unjustly accused. Apparently, I bring mud into the house.'

'Never!'

'Allegedly, I leave my smelly dirty clothes all over the place. It is said that my room's a tip.'

'Tell your social worker.'

'Haven't got one,' he said.

'Tell *my* social worker. No, don't bother. She's useless.'

'You get all the luck,' he said. 'I *never* had a social worker.' He pretended to cry.

She punched his chest. 'I bet what Becky says is all true... about you being impossible to live with.' She fell silent, wondering if he was.

They were walking back from the car park, at the end of another school day. It was hot. Their shirts were sticking to their backs, and Gwynedd had the sensation that her body was simply a machine for producing sweat. She could feel it trickling down into the hollow at the bottom of her back, and then over her bum. She could see the sweat trickling down Sam's forehead. Funny how the body passed through different ages, producing different things. In babyhood, it produced poo and wee and sick; she knew that from seeing her mate Lynn's older sister with the baby she'd had last year. She'd watched the mother wipe it and wash it and powder it and make it smell lovely, and then she'd watched the baby machine start up again and produce more poo and wee and sick. One day, her own body would turn into a machine for producing babies. All the older girls that didn't get away from the town seemed to produce a baby within two years of leaving school. It just happened. After that, male and female seemed to produce a crop of illnesses and aches and pains, and ended up old.

'I don't know why mum goes on and on,' said Sam, going on and on. 'Nobody's so much as shoved their nose through the door so far, and when they do, it won't be unannounced. There'll be a warning. That's what estate agents are for.'

But there wasn't any warning. Prospective buyers arrived out of the blue one Saturday morning, and Gwynedd was there to see them arrive. The couple pushed their way into the cottage, the man using his fat frame, the woman her bony elbows. Once inside, the man expressed delight at everything he saw. He was overpowering in his larger than life enthusiasm. Gwynedd noted his greasiness, and picked up the smell of animals that clung to his clothes. It wasn't the fresh air smell of sheep and cow that local farmers gave off, more the fetid scent of zoos and circuses, places where animals were kept in captivity. There were other things she didn't like...the thin grey pony-tail that oiled its way down his back, and the look of the bully in the way he walked, the cunning that lurked behind his eyes. She didn't like his loud voice and bad breath, and the total absence of mirth in the face of a man who laboured so hard to make jokes all the blooming time.

The man loomed over Becky. 'This your young man?' he said, grasping Sam by the arm and hand. 'Pleased to meet you. Now, who do you put me in mind of? I know, that handsome bloke on the telly that advertises those French cars - the one the women all roll their eyes at. This the sitting room? Cosy. Nice and cosy. Suit us, eh, Mags? Open fire – I like that. It's like the heart of a home, isn't it? I can see us settled in here, Mags. You with your pipe and me with my knitting. I'm only joking. You have to treat life as a laugh, don't you? Stark, staring, bleeding tragedy otherwise. This the kitchen...?'

'No,' said Sam. 'We keep the cooker and the sink in it because there isn't room in the shed.'

'Sam! Don't be so rude.' Becky was flustered.

'He's a lad,' said the man. 'Nothing rude in that. I was one myself once.'

'He was an' all,' said the woman he'd called "Mags". 'Hard to believe, I know, but there's photos.'

Gwynedd took Sam's arm to lead him out of the kitchen, to escape the smell and the man's overbearing presence, but Mags blocked the doorway. God almighty, Gwynedd thought, what have we got here? A spike by the look of it – or maybe a walking hypodermic. Long and thin, and with a sack of poison in her entrails. What's happened to her face? Gone sour. Too much thunder in the air, and too much acid in the gut. What's she been using for make-up? Chili powder for lipstick – how else did she get that blistered look on her lips, like when you deep fry bits of batter. It's a tart's face with a tart's look on it. Fine if you like studs in the ears, rings in the nose, safety pins in the throat. There's something in it reminds you of something, though, ain't there, girl. Yeah, an anteater with a pain in its guts. No, it reminds you of someone.

40

You mean there's two people look like that? What a cruel world!

'You're the son, then,' said Mags to Sam, as though he wasn't far short of a national disaster. 'I always loved children.' The voice made the words totally unconvincing. 'Loved to have had more of them myself, but Len wasn't up to it.'

While her Len lumbered from room to room, Mags remained statuesquely still, with her arms folded in front of her in what she clearly considered a graceful pose. So it was Len who led the way upstairs, calling first at the bathroom. 'The usual offices,' he said cheerily. 'It'll be a change to go indoors, eh, Mags?' He crashed on into Becky's bedroom.

'Live local, do you?' said Gwynedd. Where had she seen eyes like that before?

'We're practically neighbours,' said Mags, with a touch of hurt surprise in her voice, as though she and her bloke were key players on the social scene. 'Up the road.' She waved her hand in the vague direction of north, where the Wye valley narrowed before opening out to encompass the little town of Rhayader.

And then Gwynedd realised who they were – the Mangles. It was the local name for them, that she'd first heard from Dave, who'd first heard it from the landlord of *The Castle Inn*, who'd first heard it from a tipsy teacher who was fond of anagrams - a mixed-up version of the letters of the couples' first names... Len and Mags. Gwynedd gasped. Now she had it. Now she knew where she'd seen something that looked like this Mags's face. The same ferrety features were stuck on the front of Mollie's head. These weirdos must be Mollie's parents – the couple who'd come to Rhayader eighteen months ago and settled down to make their home in two decaying removal trucks and an old camper van in the middle of a pine forest. Gossip had it that everything rotted there – motors, fridges, old TVs, cans. Unwanted debris of plastic and polystyrene slowly settled into the undergrowth, and carrier bags wrapped themselves round trees. Piles of empty bottles and crusty rusty tins obliterated the ecological landscape. But no one went near them to complain, for their compound was guarded by an unknown number of fierce dogs, reputedly killers. Mr and Mrs Franklin, they called themselves - though some said that wasn't their real name - and they claimed to be "dealers", but nobody knew what they dealt in and nobody dared to ask. Beyond the wood, there was a small tract of land where it was rumoured they grew dope – some said for sale, some said for their own use, some said to mix in their dogs' feed, to keep the beasts under sedated control. There were hundreds of stories about them, for local imagination loved to run riot. The Mangles were never seen in town. Where they went to shop, drink, have their hair done, chew the fat or get their tablets, nobody knew. But here was a bit of information to store up for later use... beneath all that hair styling and bling and fancy fashion accessories, Mollie and her family lived like tramps.

'And who are you?' said Mags. 'The hired help?'

'She's a friend,' said Sam.

'I see. Like that, is it? Should have thought a handsome young man like you could have found himself something better. No offence, dear,' she added, twitching a grim little smile at Gwynedd.

'Oh, I say,' shouted Len, for he had blundered into Sam's room. 'This is what I call a real boy's den!'

'Lucky little beggar, aren't you,' said Mrs Franklin, as though a grave injustice had been done in giving Sam a room.

'I'm afraid it's not very tidy at the moment,' said Becky.

'Lived in,' announced Len. 'As a room should be. I don't believe in tidiness. Betrays too much self-control. I'm not one for self-control.'

'Huh!' exclaimed Mrs Franklin.

'Life's for living. Furniture's for using, not for dusting or primping. A place for everything and nothing in its place, that's me. Well, I must say, your little castle has taken my heart. What's the asking price?'

Becky told him. He looked at his wife. 'What d'you reckon, Mags?'

'Knock off twenty-five grand, because they always ask too much,' she replied. 'No offence, love, but we're business people ourselves and we know how business works.'

Becky put her hand to her heart, as though she was finding breathing difficult. 'Will you have a survey done?'

'Tell you what – knock off twenty-five grand and we won't bother with any surveyor. Nosey parkers, creeping round other people's property. I'd set the dogs on them.'

'He would and all,' said Mrs Franklin.

'How about it?'

'Could I have a day or two to think it over?'

Gwynedd stared at Becky. The poor woman was not happy. Didn't like being rushed into a deal even though she's desperate to go to Bristol and live with her fancy man. And never mind her. Look at Sam's face. He ain't got no choice. That's the trouble with adults – they keep going on about how their children come first, but not when there's choices to be made. That's when they make all the decisions, and go off where they like, when they like.

'Think it over? No way,' said Len Franklin, without malice. 'Where would any of the world's leaders have got to if they'd thought things over? We either do the business now, or we don't bother.'

'Perhaps you'd like a cup of coffee?'

'Certainly would,' said Len, and he led the way downstairs to the kitchen. 'In here? Milk for me, milk and three sugars for the wife. Mind you, she's sweet enough, as I keep telling her...'

'That'll be the day,' said Mags.

The Franklin-Mangles sat at the table while Becky fussed with kettle and *cafétiere* to make poncy real coffee.

'What's that?' said Len, pointing at the *cafétiere*. 'A time bomb? Or something you put hamsters in when they've been naughty?'

'Len loves animals,' said Mags. 'Treats them better than he does children.'

'But what is it?' Len was frowning.

'It's a *cafétiere*,' said Becky.

'Oh, pardonnez-moi,' said Len. 'That'll have put five K on the price of the cottage, eh, Mags?'

While Sam hung around in the doorway, Gwynedd shoved herself forward, to take the last chair at the table. A chance to make a close inspection of Mollie's parents – this was too good to miss.

'As to payment,' said Len. 'No problem. I've got the deposit here...' He produced a roll of soiled fifty pound notes snapped together with an elastic band that had the tension of a gin trap. '...and we'll find some blood-sucking building society to do the rest. It'll be the first time in my life I've ever owed money, but when I heard your place was on the market, I was set on having it. Neighbouring property, you see. Can't pass up a chance like that. And Mags won't last much longer in that old van of ours.'

'It's the rats,' explained Mags. 'I don't mind the noise. It's finding them on the bed. And when they run up and down the sleeves of my negligees.' She twitched a smile of feminine solidarity at Becky. 'If only Len'd let the dogs loose, we wouldn't have a rat for miles around.'

'Or a sheep. Or a postman. Or a copper! That's the trouble. They're too lively, my dogs. Got a spirit you'd never be able to beat out of them. Got to keep 'em under control. Let 'em know who's boss.'

'He loves dogs,' said Mags. 'He feels about dogs like

45

I do about chocolate.'

'I *do* love dogs,' said her husband. 'And they love me. I call to them. It's a gift.'

'Pity he's not the same with humans. He don't call to many of them.' She turned to Sam. 'Here – you must know my Mollie. Of course you do... Sam! Yes, of course. She's always talking about you. You're a naughty boy, aren't you? Bit forward. Can't leave my babe alone, from what I hear.' She glanced at Gwynedd. 'So who are you?'

'Sam's girlfriend,' said Gwynedd.

'Don't think so, love. According to my babe, Sam's already spoken for. Still, no shame in coming second.'

Becky served the coffee and stood awkwardly behind Gwynedd. The Franklin-Mangles blew noisily on their mugs and conversation momentarily died. Sam was about to withdraw, when the back door crashed open and Ben bounded in, stone in mouth. Tail wagging, eyes gleaming, and with his usual acceptance of everyone and everything as a present from heaven, the dog nosed up to Len Franklin, and solemnly offered the complete stranger his stone. It was Ben's favourite stone, the one he slept on.

'Watch this,' said Mag. 'He'll have that dog a lifelong friend before you could say "Kill".'

'Ben's like that with everyone,' said Sam, with just a touch of anger in his voice.

'So it's Ben, is it?' said Len. 'Fine name for a fine dog. And you're moving home, eh, Ben? And where are you off to?'

'That's a bit of a problem,' said Becky. 'Sam and I are going to Bristol. To a flat. And Ben can't come with us. It's a bit of a worry. In fact, if you know of anyone...'

Len's coffee mug crashed to the table. 'Are you blind, dear?' he said to her. 'What do I look like? Not wearing dog skin trousers, am I? Here, Mags, you're not flaunting a dog's-tooth necklace, by any chance? Dog-lovers? That's what I've got in mind to have chiselled on my gravestone. "Here lies Len Franklin, dog-lover".'

'If I'm still alive, I'll add a little footnote,' said Mags, and again Gwynedd saw her wink at Becky.

'You mean, you'd be prepared to take him?'

'Looks to me like he's already made up his mind, eh, boy?' Len Franklin bent down and patted Ben's flank. The dog dropped his favourite stone, gyrated happily and licked the man's vast hand. 'It *is* a gift. I love dogs and dogs love me.'

'You've got to let him stay with Len and me,' said Mags. 'Don't want *unnecessary* suffering, do we? He'll have the time of his life with us. The run of the whole farm.'

Gwynedd snorted. Farm! That camp of the Mangles! That rubbish tip, spewing out filth and muck and stink. They got stuff there a land-fill site wouldn't take. But Becky won't see it that way. She'll believe it's a better place for Ben than a flat in Bristol. She'll have to believe that because she wants to be shot of Ben. Poor Sam, he'll have his beloved Ben handed over to a couple of smelly cranks. Worse than that... Ben'll be handed over to Mollie's parents. That'll give the cow a real hold over Sam.

'That's settled then. I reckon we've struck a bargain here this morning, Mags. A pretty cottage and a lovely dog. Drink up your coffee, my angel, while I pay our charming hostess the deposit on our new home.' Len Franklin dug deep into the pocket of his combat fatigue trousers, and the roll of notes appeared again. He peeled off a hundred of them, placing them in piles of ten on the table. Gwynedd looked at the piles, and tried to calculate how many weeks, months, years of housekeeping money lay within her reach.

'Hadn't we better talk to the agent?' Becky suggested, nervously.

'Agents! Not much of a-*gent* about those bastards... I beg your pardon, your ladyship. Just a slip of the tongue. I hope you and your cafeterereria haven't taken offence.'

'He calls it slip of the tongue,' said Mags. 'I call it bleeding crude.'

'You'll have to forgive my little jokes,' said Len. 'But where would we be without a sense of humour? It's what I call the Great Relaxative.'

'That's what first attracted me to Len,' said Mags. 'A sense of humour - mine, unfortunately.'

'Perhaps it would be better to talk to a solicitor,' said Becky. The piles of notes were mounting. 'I mean, I wouldn't be happy with all that cash lying about the house the whole weekend.'

Len stopped counting and looked up. He frowned. 'What you need's a good guard dog. A real killer. One that would make an unwelcome guest practically

48

fill his...'

'They're moving, Len,' said Mags. 'That's why we're taking this one off their hands.'

'Of course, of course,' said Len. 'What am I thinking of?' His hand hovered over the money for a moment, as though he was unsure what to do. Then he snatched up the five thousand pounds and shoved it back in his combat fatigues. He got up and held out his hand to Becky. 'Of course I couldn't let a lovely lady like you run the risk of having your house broken into, and some violent sod...'

'Language, Len,' warned his wife.

'Don't you stop me in full flow, Mags. Remember last time? We don't want *that* again. No, the money will be perfectly safe with me, and I'll be at that grasping, blood-sucking agent's first thing Monday. So, what's yer name, darling?'

'Harper,' said Becky. 'Becky Harper.'

'Rebecca,' said Len. 'Lovely name. Literary. Biblical. And with a lilt to it. It's a real pleasure to do business with you, Rebecca. And with you, too, sir.' He turned to Sam. 'And with you also, Ben.' He held out a hand, into which Ben obligingly placed his paw.

'Look at that! We're made for each other, Ben and me.' He made a lot of laughter go a very long way.

As she left, Mrs Franklin-Mangles gave Gwynedd a quick and chilling inspection from head to toe, but said nothing. And then they were gone.

Becky looked at Sam. Sam kept his eyes determinedly on Ben. Neither of them looked at Gwynedd.

'I know you don't want to move, love,' said Becky. 'But I do. I know you want to stay here, but we can't. We're moving and that's it...'

Gwynedd couldn't hold back. The thought of Ben bringing Sam and Mollie together was getting on her nerves. 'You're not thinking about this, Becky. It's not right. You let them Mangles bully you into doing what they wanted. Suppose someone turns up tomorrow – someone who wouldn't turn this place into a junkyard? You wouldn't dream of selling to the Mangles then, would you?'

'I don't know what you mean by the Mangles. The point is, these people *have* turned up. Nobody else has. They've made an offer. Nobody else has. Nobody in town can afford this place – there isn't the money around. No one else local will buy this. And no tourist or holiday-maker is going to fall in love with it. You're about the only person who so much as passes it. Those two are the only customers I'll get. I have to sell to them.' There were tears in Becky's eyes.

Yeah, so what? Becky's crying because life don't give her *all* she wants. So what? That *is* life. You don't get what you want from life – not the big things. You get sweets and balloons when you're a kid, smokes and booze when you're grown-up. And that's about it. But did that mean Becky shouldn't get what she wanted, if she could? You can't be a spoilsport in life and say nobody should get what they want because you don't. Never mind about me, thought Gwynedd. This isn't about me. It's about Sam. Look at him, pacing round the kitchen in them shorts that show off his lovely legs, and that T shirt that's just the right blue for him. He's lovely. Yeah, but the point is, he's unhappy. And if Becky gets what she wants, he'll be even more unhappy. Something would have to be done, but since it involved Mollie's parents, it would take a lot of sorting out.

It was time to be off. There was the weekend shopping to do and then Dave's dinner to get. 'Coming up town?' she said.

'Yeah,' said Sam.

'You go, Gwynedd. Sam will join you in a little while,' said Becky. 'I'd like a word with him first.'

Gwynedd left them to it, and set off for Rhayader. She'd got plenty on her mind, and all of it was to do with the Franklin-Mangles. There was money there. Loads of it. That wad of notes... where did that come from? Where had Len earned that? Building trade? Car dealing? Could be, there were lots of dodgy dealers in both those games. It had to be something physical. There was no way Len Franklin spent his working days behind a desk. Nobody who worked in a shop or an office ended up with a weather-beaten face like that. He could be a thief. He could be a copper. One thing was for sure – he wasn't the sort of bloke to get on the wrong side of.

Then there was Mollie. Gwynedd couldn't wait for Monday to come round so that she could make use of what she'd learned about Mollie's family. Mollie Pryce? Maybe. Mollie Franklin? More likely. But whoever she was, she lived in a dump. So, roll on, Monday morning.

First thing, on the school bus, Gwynedd would tell everyone all about the real Mollie. She'd tease her, taunt her, expose her, make every ride to and from school such a nightmare for Mollie that she wouldn't dare show her face ever again. Gwynedd would get rid of her, and enjoy doing it. It would be like digging a splinter out from under your fingernail. Finding a way to drive Mollie out of her life was what Gwynedd had been praying for ever since the bitch had first appeared.

Only when she reached the town did it occur to Gwynedd that getting rid of Mollie wouldn't do anything to stop Sam going to Bristol. She suddenly felt the need to have a little with chat with her doll Sasha once again. Bloody hell, would Sam feel like this when he moved to Bristol? No way. She looked around her at the grey town. Life had to be better in Bristol. Bristol had everything and this place had nothing... except some one who was fond of him. Not that he'd notice a little thing like that. If he did go to Bristol, all he'd miss was his precious Ben. And Ben was all that Sam would leave behind him, here. Which was why she'd keep an eye on Ben, and on the strange couple that were going to be Ben's new owners... for Sam's sake.

CHAPTER 5

Monday morning. Gwynedd was dressed and seated at the little table in her room, doing her face. She'd woken at dawn, after a bad night and immediately thought about the Mangles. Len was a bully. Mags was creepy. Both were sinister. There was something about their attitude to Ben that rang false, something that frightened her. The more she thought about it, the more she was convinced that some harm might come to Ben. And then her thoughts turned to Mollie living in Sam's cottage once he and Becky had moved to Bristol. Mollie would sleep in what was now Sam's room. She'd lie there in bed looking at Sam's ceiling. She'd look out of his windows. There'd be Mollie's clothes in Sam's cupboard, the one tucked under the eaves. Gwynedd remembered how Sam had once threatened, years ago, to lock her in that cupboard, when her teasing had got up his nose. Those were good days, but there'd be no knocking on the cottage door once Sam was gone. No tiptoeing to the window to see what was going on inside, not with Len and Mags and

Mollie living there. Well, never mind all that. The good thing was, today was the day Mollie Franklin was going to get what she'd been asking for.

'Where's my bloody breakfast!' That was Dave, outside her bedroom door.

'You don't have to bloody shout!' she shouted.

She leapt up from the table and pulled on her school trousers. She'd given up wearing skirts since her first fight with Mollie, months back. You can't fight well in a skirt. She screwed what was left of her obligatory school tie into a knot round her throat and buttoned her shirt, grabbed her shoes and wrenched the door open.

'Move it, Dave,' she shouted as she dashed to the kitchen. He followed her, which usually meant he had something on his mind.

'Just give us beans on toast,' he said.

That was a relief. Beans on toast wouldn't take two minutes and she was already behind schedule.

'Going on a diet?'

'No, no,' he said. 'It's just... well, they was saying on the TV yesterday... some doctor... beans is good for you.'

'Beans, beans are good for your heart...' Gwynedd started on the old chant as she cut the bread for his toast.

He interrupted her. 'That's what this doc said... good for the heart. Don't bother with butter on the toast, love. Just the beans. And bring it through to the front room, will you?' He left the kitchen.

'I always do,' she shouted. 'Haven't you noticed?'

Five minutes later she was racing across the fields to meet up with Sam. She found him sitting on one of the swings with a frown on his face.

'Spit it out,' she said, 'and then we can plan exactly how we're going to ruin Mollie's day.'

'Mum wants to go to Bristol a week on Thursday. Spend a night there. Have a look at this flat we'll be living in. Martin's arranged it all.'

'What's this Martin like?'

'He's a wet.'

'Well then, he doesn't matter, does he? So when your mum goes to spend a night with him…'

'Don't be daft. She's not going for that. She's going to find a school for me.'

'Oh, yeah! You know a lot about life, don't you! She wants a night out with this Martin. Wining and dining and then… Don't look so shocked. It's perfectly normal, and legal, for a man and woman to spend the night together. It might even happen to you… one night… if you found someone daft enough.' She laughed gently at the horror on his face and impulsively leant towards him and kissed his cheek. 'Anyway, when she goes – whatever she goes for – you come and stay at our place. I'll cook you a smashin' tea.' She felt excited. This was going to be a really good day.

'Well, Mum's already making arrangements for me to go and stay at Huwie's, with his parents.'

'With Huwie? You've got to be joking. You can't go and stay there. It'll be horrible. You'll have to be polite all the time, and sit up nicely, and use a knife and fork. You tell your Mum you're coming to stay with me... and that's an order.'

'Mum will want to check it out with Dave. I can't just tell her. She'll insist on writing him a letter, to thank him in advance. She's probably written to Huwie's mum and dad already.' There was doubt in his voice.

'What!' She looked at him as though he was mad. 'Dave can't know anything about this. He'd say "no" to it if he did! We don't say anything to him until you arrive on the doorstep Thursday night next week, and then there's bloody nothing he can do about it.'

'You want me to lie to my mum.'

'Oh, for goodness sake! Just don't tell her the truth.'

'And if I do that and she phones Huwie's mum and dad from Bristol to check I'm OK and I'm not there, she'll have a fit.'

Gwynedd frowned, but only for a moment, then her face brightened. 'No problem. Get her to give you a note to give to me to give to Dave, asking if you can come and stay with us. There's no way he'll get it. Don't look so worried, your ma will get a reply – an' a much better one than Dave could ever write.' She smiled at the bewilderment on his face. 'From me. She'll get a reply from me.'

'Supposing mum posts a letter to Dave?'

'Still no problem. I'll have a word with Postman Pat. Get him to put it in my private mailbox – like he does the letters of complaint from school. He does anything I want – he has to, since he made the mistake of trying to get me to pose for his fancy home videos. So… you are coming to stay then? I knew you would.' She grabbed his school bag and pulled him towards her. The movement was unexpected. He had no time to resist, but he could see what was coming and was able to turn his head just enough to receive her kiss on his ear rather than his mouth.

'Now, about Mollie,' she said. 'Today's the day we ruin her life.'

'What do you mean?'

'Make an announcement to everyone on the bus about her and her parents and where they live. Shame her. Totally shame her!'

Sam frowned. 'You can't.'

'Why not?'

'You approve of bullies, do you?'

'Course not. You know I don't. I hate them. I want to punch them in their ugly mugs…'

'So why be a bully yourself?'

'I'm not being a bully. I'm just telling everyone the truth about that cow Mollie.'

'She can't help where she lives or who her parents are. It's not her fault.'

The really good day turned sour. 'So you're on her side?'

He avoided the question. 'We're going to miss the bus if we don't go now.' He set off.

She followed, arguing. 'I don't understand,' she said. 'Mollie Pryce or Mollie Franklin or whatever she's bloody called, is a cow. Don't you see that?'

He didn't answer, but hurried on, out of the park and across the road to the car park. She clattered after him. The bus was very near now, its engine ticking over.

'I'm talking to you,' she shouted.

Sam got on the bus. She followed, too angry to say what was in her head. He fancied Mollie. That was it. Instead of the cow getting what she deserved, she'd got what she wanted. She'd got a hold over him. He was protecting her. The worst part of it was that, deep inside, Gwynedd reckoned he was right. Exposing Mollie would be bullying. It didn't help that Sam had shown that she was wrong to be gunning for Mollie. And there was the cow, smiling at him, acting like she owned him.

The bus started up, and headed out of the town.

'Hello, Sammy, darling. Come up here. Sit with us.'

The words were addressed to Sam, but Mollie's eyes were on Gwynedd. There were a few titters from Mollie's cronies.

Gwynedd reminded herself that she had everything under control; she knew something the others didn't know. This was going to be a moment of glory. She turned on Mollie. 'I know all about you, so you can shut your gob.'

'Not very ladylike, Sammy, is she?' Mollie grabbed Sam's arm and pulled him into the seat beside her.

The moment of glory vanished. Gwynedd was up on her feet.

Sam tried to restrain her. 'No,' he said. 'Leave it.

Please leave it!'

She shook herself free. 'You keep out of this. I can fight my own battles.'

'Why does it always have to be a battle?'

'Because it bloody does,' Gwynedd snapped. She took a couple of quick steps down the middle of the bus and then leant across and swung Sam's bag into Mollie's face. The bus erupted with joy, but the fight was short. The driver slammed on the brakes, left his seat, and forced his way between the two girls. It took all his strength to bundle Gwynedd into the nearest empty seat.

'That's assault!' she snarled.

'You control yourself or you're off this bus.' The driver was shaking and gulping great mouthfuls of air. Sam feared the old man was going to have a heart attack.

'Go piss your pants,' said Gwynedd. 'I'm off anyway.' She pushed the driver aside, kicked open the bus doors, and burst out on to the side of the road.

The doors swung shut. The bus pulled away. Sam twisted round in his seat and saw Gwynedd stick two fingers up at the bus, turn on her heel, and begin a defiantly jaunty walk back towards Rhayader. He also saw that she still had his bag in her hand.

CHAPTER 6

'I told you – we've all been sent home. There's no water at school.' Gwynedd had invented the lie on her trudge back to Rhayader, for the jaunty walk had lasted only as long as the school bus was still in sight. 'Go on then - phone them if you don't believe me!' She brandished her mobile in Dave's face. She hadn't found the money to top it up, but it didn't matter if he called her bluff. He didn't know how to use it anyway.

'But you're all right?'

She nodded, surprised. What was this? He'd never asked if she was all right before.

'Can you cook the dinner then? Save me bothering?'

So that was why he asked. She should have guessed.

Her bad mood lasted all morning. She tidied her room, cleaned the kitchen, and cooked Dave's dinner.

'You'll be here to get my tea?' There was anxiety in his voice. 'Just because you cooked dinner don't mean you won't cook tea?'

'Don't worry. I'll cook your bloomin' tea.' Great life this was; an unexpected day off school and nothing to do. She needed Sam, but he was back at school, being a goodie-goodie. He should have followed her off the bus. They could be having a good time together, right now. Instead of which, she was stuck with Dave, and Sam was no doubt being chatted up by that cow Mollie.

Gwynedd sat on her bed. Nearly three, and Sam wouldn't be along to pick up his bag until half past four at the earliest. She could go and wait for him at the car park, but not for as long as an hour and a half. There was the Paki lad in the chippie. She could go and flirt with him but, for some reason she didn't understand, that didn't appeal right now. She lay back on the bed and gazed at the ceiling.

Mollie! It was all that stupid cow's fault. Her and her parents. If the Mangles hadn't come along wanting to buy Becky's cottage, Sam wouldn't be moving to Bristol and everything would be all right. Somebody ought to teach those Mangles a lesson. They were up to something out there in the woods, and where did all that money come from? It would be fun to sneak out there sometime and have a good nose around. Everyone talked about there being dangerous dogs out there... why would the Mangles have savage dogs unless they had something to hide? If it was possible to find out what was going on, maybe she'd be in a position to tell Mollie to keep off Sam or risk exposure. And, at the same time, it would be good ammunition to use against Sam to stop him sticking up for Mollie. Better than that, maybe she'd be in a position to put paid to the Mangles' plan to buy the cottage. That was all going through much too fast. There was talk of the Mangles moving in during the summer holidays.

The more she thought about it, the more the idea of spying on the Mangles appealed to her. She wondered why she hadn't thought of it before. How long would it take to get to the woods, find out what was going on, and get back? Two hours? More like three. And what was the time now? Half past three. No chance to get there and back before Sam came round. So why not wait? Get him to go with her. She'd get Dave's tea early, and then she and Sam would set off. Sam would be scared, of course, but that would be half the fun. Right, that was settled!

She leapt up from her bed. The first thing to do was to prepare her combat gear. She rummaged in the bottom drawer of her wardrobe, and pulled out a dark sweater, a pair of baggy old trousers, and her heaviest boots. She piled them on the floor by her bed, and added a black woolly hat from a hook on the back of her bedroom door. What else would she need? Camouflage, since this was going to be an SAS style operation. She'd get that from the kitchen, later. Meantime, she'd have another little lie on the bed, a little rest. There was a lot to be done tonight.

Dave's voice woke her. He was shouting from the passage.

'Someone to see you!'

Again, she leapt off the bed. That'd be Sam. He'd come to see her, and she had to get to him quick to tell him about the raid on the Mangles' camp, and to stop him saying anything to Dave about what happened on the school bus. She yanked open her bedroom door, and raced to the front door. But it wasn't Sam, it was Skinny Vinnie.

'Just thought I'd pop in, like, to see that you were okey-dokey,' he said, and gave her one of his lop-sided grins.

'And what's all this about you being slung off the bus?' said Dave. 'You better have some good explanation ready when you bring me my tea... ' He shuffled into the front room, back to his beloved telly.

'I was just telling your granddad all about it,' said Vinnie, as she led him to the kitchen. 'He pretended he was getting furious about it. I had a good laugh. He's all right, isn't he. Bit of a character, like.'

'Vinnie, you're such a pain in the backside.'

It seemed to Vinnie that he wasn't really wanted. 'Righto,' he said. 'I'll nip out and pop back later, then. Here, Gwen, guess what. I'm getting a bike. You know, a proper bike. It's got a proper engine and everything, and you have to take a test.'

'So, when's all this happening?' Gwynedd found it hard to be angry with Vinnie for long.

'7th March. My birthday. Pisces.'

'That's months away.'

'It's gotta come though, hasn't it? That's the whole point about life. It's gotta come. *Que sera, sera*.'

Too bloody true, but right now she had to get rid of Vinnie.

'Thanks for calling,' she said, 'only right now I got to get my grandad's tea. So, cheers, Vinnie, mind you don't cut yourself on that razor sharp wit of yours.'

She marched him to the door. It was bad timing. Sam was coming up the path.

The row was short and sharp. Vinnie took no part in it. He was used to being given a verbal bum rush from many places, and left with scarcely a murmur. But Sam was angry that he'd had to walk all the way up to Gwynedd's bungalow to get his bag, and even more angry to see Vinnie coming out of the bungalow with a smirk on his face. On top of which, he didn't know what to say when Dave started asking questions about what had or hadn't gone wrong with the water supply at school. Within five minutes, Sam was on his way back downhill to his cottage, and Gwynedd's plans for an evening together were ruined.

She, too, was angry, but she saw no reason for cancelling the trip to the Mangles' camp. She'd go on her own. She half-convinced herself that she'd prefer to go on her own. She got Dave's tea - a bit of ham and salad and a large pile of bread and butter - collected her camouflage from the kitchen, and then settled down in her bedroom to wait until he was deep into an evening of television. Sitting in front of her mirror, she smeared brown sauce and mushy peas over her face. Given the colour of her skin there was really no need, but that simply made it all the more enjoyable. There! Finished. Better than any undercover agent.

She changed into her combat gear, shoved her

woolly hat into her pocket, stuck her heaviest boots under her arm, and slipped out by the back door. Once she was down the garden, she sat on Dave's beloved compost heap and pulled on her boots.

It was a warm evening, with the sun already hidden by the mountains, the faintest of July moons low in the sky, and a light breeze blowing. She decided on a roundabout route to the forest, crouching low and using the cover of hedges and walls wherever possible, while it was still light. There was always the risk that she might be spotted by some old nosey, with nothing better to do than spend all day spying from her front room window. But once she'd crossed a couple of fields, there was no risk of being seen, and the going was easier. Gwynedd moved swiftly and silently over the soft springy turf. Within minutes she reached the edge of the pine forest.

Once into the trees, she stopped to get her breath back and to wipe the sweat out of her eyes. She sniffed the air like an animal, and listened. There was no sound, and when she sniffed all she could smell was the soft scent of the pines, with just a hint of brown sauce and mushy peas. OK, time to move on, but careful now. Step on a bit of dead wood and it would snap with a crack like a gun going off.

It was dark in the pines. Even on sunny days, little light or heat penetrated the branches above her, and a gloomy air hung about the place. You betcha there was something strange going on here. You betcha the Mangles were up to something dirty. And what a tale she'd have to tell Sam.

Gwynedd moved on, slipping from tree to tree, pausing for a while behind each one, checking that all was well. But the forest was large, her progress was slow, and she became impatient. She hurried on and came to a small clearing in the wood, roughly circular in shape, where a dozen or more trees had been hacked down. Here the scent of pines gave way to a musty smell of decay and rot and mould. Creepy. It was a good job she didn't have Little Huwie's wild imagination. He'd have seen witches and banshees behind every bloody pine and then freaked out and had a fit. You couldn't bring him here. But you could bring Sam. That'd be good. Get him away from thoughts of Bristol and bring him to the Enchanted Wood... the Beautiful Princess leading the Gallant Knight, taking him to challenge the Wicked Old Cow of the Woods, formerly known as Mollie Pryce.

As she worked her way round the edge of the clearing, she sensed rather than saw a slight movement in the trees above. She looked up. It was all she could do not to scream. Hanging from a dead pine were the remains of two corpses... a pair of foxes. The beasts had been shot – she could see the wounds where the gunshot had peppered their heads and flanks – and then strung up by their hind legs. The corpses had putrefied, and she guessed the slaughter had taken place some time ago. That thought helped her to stay put, and not turn tail to make a run for home. Keep going, she told herself. They're only dead foxes. Someone blown them away with a gun, happens all the time. Quickest way to deal with the vermin. Farmers do it every week.

But for once her inner voice lacked conviction. These beasts had not been killed in an ordinary fox shoot. There was something weird and frightening about the way the bodies had been suspended from the dead pine – almost as though they were sacrifices at some sort of ritual. Almost as if they were hanging from a fox gibbet, a place of execution. She forced herself to move closer, to get a better look. The fur on their backs had lost its warm, rusty colour and glossy tone. Their brushes hung limp and bedraggled down their backs. The teeth of both were bared, showing through the flesh that had shrunk and tightened round their leering mouths. It was grotesque, as though they were laughing at their own deaths.

It was a point of honour with Gwynedd never to shirk a challenge, so she made herself inspect the hideous spectacle more closely still. Then she realised that some other animal had been at work here, gnawing at the carcasses, for the bellies had been ripped open and chunks of flesh torn away. The smell was bad, and the nests of maggots breeding inside the bodies made her feel sick. She staggered back into the shelter of the trees. No matter how hard she tried she couldn't stop herself coughing and retching. The noise seemed absurdly, dangerously loud.

'Shut up,' she hissed to herself, and then coughed some more.

She waited as long as she dared, listening intently and looking about her. She felt cold now, for the sweat had soaked into her clothing and she was losing body heat. She shivered again. There was no sound. Perhaps she was safe. She continued her examination of the grim scene and noticed strange marks on some of the trees near the fox gibbet. The other animal – whatever it was – had been here, too. There were gashes on the trunks of the pines. Bits of broken bough littered the ground, scarred with teeth marks and claw marks, from something a sight bigger than a fox. Not a badger, she thought. The marks on the trees were too high from the ground for a badger. And not a squirrel, unless it was a bloody giant squirrel. What then?

The answer to her question came as she asked it. From deeper in the forest she heard the barking of dogs, a deep and hungry noise that challenged her courage. That'll do, she decided. Time to go. For all she knew, the Mangles might have dogs loose in the wood. For all she knew some hound the size of a bloody pony might come bounding into the clearing any moment.

But Gwynedd moved cautiously on. It began to get dark. She wondered how much further she had to go. Surely she was near the centre of the forest by now. And then she saw the twin beams of headlamps flashing through the trees ahead and heard the grind of a car engine. A vehicle was jolting its way slowly up some sort of track. Someone was busy even at this hour of night.

CHAPTER 7

She almost blundered into a pile of rubbish - rusting cans, plastic bottles, broken glass, and old food packets – and knew that she must be getting very near to the camp. She could hear the dogs now – two at least, possibly a third. The barking was deep throated, like it came from empty, hungry bellies, and immediately she felt the urge to run away. She fought it, cursing herself under her breath and telling herself not to be such a baby. She hadn't come out for a pleasant stroll in the woods, but for adventure. This was a secret that no one else was in on. *She* had to find out what the Mangles were up to, and then she'd have to keep that secret to herself. There could be no sharing this with Sam, not if it was to do with dogs, not if it involved any kind of danger for Ben. Poor Sam – if he'd been here, he'd be wetting himself by now.

She heard the vehicle stop. The lights went out. Two doors slammed, and she heard someone swearing at the dogs and telling them to 'shut it!' The dogs did as they were told. She guessed it was the Mangles returning home, and knew she was right when she heard the rasping voice of Mags.

'Shut it, the lot of you! I swear to God, Len, one of these days I'll wire up their chains to the generator...'

'You've got to love them, Magsie.' That was Len. 'And to do that, you've got to understand them. Born and raised to kill.' His voice was louder now, as if Mags was some distance off. 'What d'you expect? Wagging tails and a soft wet tongue on the back of your hand? Anyone trying that with you, Prince, would be lucky to keep their hand, eh, boy?'

Gwynedd decided that she had to get just that little bit nearer to find out exactly what was going on. She dropped on to her stomach, and snaked her way from tree to tree, round the piles of rubbish, till she reached the edge of a much larger clearing, the heart of the Mangles camp. Set among the trees and stunted bushes were three removal trucks and a caravan. She crept closer, as near as she dared, and crouched down behind a clump of bramble, bracing herself for instant flight. This was scary, all right, for she doubted her ability to outrun a dog. But she was determined to see it through. This was the Mangles' camp. This was where whatever they were up to took place. Now she had the chance to find out exactly what that was.

It sounded as though Len was fumbling with some kind of lock that fastened the back doors of one of the big removal trucks. The hinges groaned as he swung the doors open. Then he returned to the vehicle he'd arrived in, and took a crate from the back. She heard him grunt as he lifted it, and pant as he carried it along. And she heard a whimpering noise. There was something in the crate. An animal? A second dog? Then there was another grunt, as Len dropped the crate in the back of the removal truck, and what sounded like an animal yelping in pain or fear. She heard Len taunt whatever "it" was.

'You think you've got something to complain about now. You don't know what's in store, Fido.' Back he went to the other vehicle. 'Just one more,' he called to Mags. And then he said something that sounded like 'not bad for one night's haul' or, maybe, 'trawl'.

There was no answer from Mags. Gwynedd was dimly aware that the barking of the other dogs, the barking that had greeted the arrival of the Mangles, had increased, but her attention was concentrated on Len. Surely, if she risked crawling just a tiny bit nearer, she would see more and hear more, and maybe she could find out what he was doing.

Steady... steady... She pulled herself forward by her fingertips and the toes of her boots, scraping the entire length of her body along the ground... just another metre at most...

There was a noise, coming from behind her. She couldn't place it for a moment, and then she smelt the sweet-and-sour scent of a struck match. A second or two later there was a whiff of cigarette smoke. Oh my God!... Had Mags managed to creep round to cut off her retreat? Gwynedd wriggled her body round to see.

It was a mistake. She put the weight of her elbow on a stick, and the stick snapped.

She heard feet rustling through the leaves, coming towards her. Time to go, and fast. She leapt up to make a run for it, but it was too late. The smoker was upon her.

'God Almighty, Gwynedd! What are you doing here?' It was Mollie, sounding every bit as frightened as Gwynedd felt. 'Quick,' she said. 'This way – quiet as you can.' She beckoned to Gwynedd to follow her along a narrow path through the bramble patches, heading away from the camp. Gwynedd did as Mollie directed. After five minutes running and stumbling, mostly uphill, Mollie stopped.

There was no sound of Len or Mags, though the dogs were barking louder than ever down below. Mollie still had the cigarette in her hand. She sucked it as though her life depended on it, and exhaled a cloud of smoke.

'You could get yourself killed here tonight,' she said.

'Oh yeah? Who's gonna kill me? Your dad?'

'You leave my dad out of it.' After a pause, she went on: 'Anyway, he's not my dad, not my real dad. He's my step dad.'

Gwynedd had no time for sympathy. At least Mollie had a dad of some sort.

'What about your mum then?'

Mollie took another pull on her cigarette. 'You know my mum?'

Gwynedd gave a rapid account of the visit of Len and Mags to Sam's cottage.

'That'll be our cottage in a couple of months,' said Mollie. She didn't sound enthusiastic.

'Not if I've got anything to do with it...'

Mollie cut her short. 'Shut up,' she said. 'I gotta think... How about a deal? You don't say nothing about my mum and dad – not to anyone – and I won't tell them about your being here tonight.' She peered closely at Gwynedd, trying to discern Gwynedd's reaction to the offer. 'What's that on your face?' she said.

Gwynedd was sweating, and trickles of sauce and peas were running down her cheeks. 'Nothing,' she said.

Mollie wiped her finger on Gwynedd's face, and then sniffed the fingertip. 'It's food,' she said.

'That's what you think,' said Gwynedd. 'It's camouflage as a matter of fact.'

'You stupid bitch. You think this is some kind of game?'

Voices floated up from the direction of the camp. 'Mollie! Where the hell are you?'

Mollie took one last puff and looked Gwynedd straight in the face. 'Up here, dad!' she shouted. Then, quietly, she said, 'Well, is it a deal?'

Gwynedd was on the point of telling her to get stuffed and then legging it out of the woods as fast as possible. But something stopped her. It was the thought of Sam, bloomin' Sam with his rubbish about what a rotten life Mollie must have. Gwynedd didn't want to make a deal, but this deal was clearly important to Mollie. It was proof that she'd do anything to keep her Len and her Mags hidden away. They may have reckoned it was time to move out of the woods, perhaps Mollie didn't share that view.

'Mollie!' The voice was nearer now.

'Deal or no deal?' Mollie stubbed her fag out on a tree trunk. She flung the dog-end into the undergrowth.

Gwynedd said nothing. She didn't know what to say. All that came to mind was a question. 'Is your dad bringing the dogs with him?'

Mollie shook her head.

'I'm all right then,' said Gwynedd.

'Not if you don't go right now.'

They could hear Len grunting as he clambered up through the trees, sticks cracking under his boots, his breath laboured. They could see the flickering light of a torch beam. He reached them. It was too late to leg it.

'You've been smoking...' The voice was threatening, but the accusation was cut off the moment he saw Gwynedd. When he spoke again, his voice was different. No menace, but a false politeness. 'Who's this, Moll? A secret boy-friend?'

'It's just a friend from school.'

'Don't get many of your friends dropping in, do we,' said Len. 'Specially at this time of night.' He pointed the torch directly at Gwynedd's face. 'Looks like some army cadet. Well, come on lad – name, rank and number... and you'd better have a good reason for being on manoeuvres here.'

'I told you, dad, it's just a girl from school.'

'I'll talk to you later, Moll.' The menace was back in

his voice. 'A girl, is it? Ah! Someone your mother and I have had the pleasure of meeting before. Gwen, isn't it. You were at our cottage, with young Sam and the lovely Rebecca, weren't you... But, like I say, it is a bit late for visitors.'

'You all right, Len?' Mags, too, was making her way up through the wood.

'We've got company,' he called back. 'No problems. Keep Prince on his chain.'

'Can't we keep mum out of it?' said Mollie.

'You know well enough we can never keep your loving mum out of anything. Not after all she went through bringing you into this world,' said Len. The torch was still fixed on Gwynedd's face. 'Whatever's this, dear? You've made yourself up like a dog's dinner. And that's not a bad idea.' He laughed. 'I'm only kidding.'

Mags joined them. 'It's the girl that makes out she's young Sam's sweetheart, hanging around where she's not wanted. Trespassing on private property. Unless, of course, this is Mollie's doing?'

'Yes, mum,' said Mollie. 'I invited her. Sort of game. Bit of fun. Like those war games with paint-guns.'

'Don't see any signs of paint,' said Len. 'Except on your friend's face. No matter – you can explain all about it later, Moll. Right now, it's time we took this young lady home.'

'I'll find my own way back,' said Gwynedd.

'At this time of night! Never. Young lady alone... your age. Anything could happen. Strange things. Nasty things. Rotten things that would really mess you up. We'll give you a lift. No, no – I insist.'

'You don't know where I live.' Gwynedd had decided she would lead them to some other house... Little Huwie's place, or where Vinnie lived.

'Don't we?' said Len. 'That nice little bungalow just over the hills from here? Lovely little spot. Just you and your grandad. We've had our eyes on the place for quite a while. Right, Mags?'

Mags was lighting a cigarette. 'You know that old song? "*Getting to know you*"? How does it go? "*...getting to like you...*" Well, that's not true. Can't say I like you.'

They led both girls back through the woods. Mollie was told to wait in the caravan for 'mum and dad's return'. The look on Mollie's face made Gwynedd think that Sam's concern might well be justified.

Gwynedd was shoved into the back seat of the vehicle that had brought Len and Mags to the woods - a flash SUV. Mags climbed in beside her, and grabbed her arm. Len pressed the central locking button; there was no way Gwynedd could get out. She made no attempt to struggle, and nothing was said on the drive back through the woods and the town. She noted the time on the instrument panel. It was just gone midnight.

It was clear that they really did know where she lived. They drove straight up to the bungalow. The minute they arrived and Len unlocked the doors, Gwynedd clambered out. Somehow, Mags managed to get her foot hooked round Gwynedd's leg, so that Gwynedd fell out of the SUV and went sprawling on the grass at the edge of the road. Mags laughed, sat back, and lit a cigarette.

Gwynedd picked herself up. She was near tears, but she had to try to have the last word. 'I hope your bloody smokin' kills you,' she said.

The door of the SUV slammed shut. Mags pressed the button to open the window. 'Do you really, dear?' She blew smoke in Gwynedd's face. 'And is that how you feel about your Grandad? Rolling his smokes, as he calls them, and lighting up one after another in front of that cheap little TV set you got.' The woman saw the fright in Gwynedd's face. 'My Len told you we had our eyes on you. We know what's going on.'

Len opened the driver's window and joined in. 'He ought to take better care of you. All that smoke in the place can't be good for you, dear. You hear such tragic tales about passive smoking. And God forbid the old fool should accidentally set fire to the place one night. Still, you just keep out of our way, and I'm sure you'll come to no harm.'

'And what if I don't?' They couldn't grab her now. She'd leg it into the bungalow.

'That'll be the day,' said Mags. The window slid shut. The Mangles drove off.

Gwynedd let herself into the bungalow by the back door. She was exhausted, to the point where she felt physically sick. She undressed wearily, letting her clothes drop to the floor. The sweater was ruined. Her boots and jeans were covered in mud. She pulled on a T-shirt and got into bed, without bothering to wash her face or brush her teeth. She lay in the dark, shaking under the duvet. She knew it was impossible to tell anyone what had happened. The police would side with the Mangles. Dave would give her an earful and then moan at her for weeks. If her social worker - Mrs Horsfall, better known as Horseface as far as Gwynedd was concerned - if Horseface got to hear of it, she'd bundle her into care. No one would understand, not even Sam, and she couldn't tell him, anyway, because he'd want to know why she'd gone to the camp, and that would bring Ben into it. She had no evidence, no proof; she wasn't even sure just what crime she suspected the Mangles were planning.

But, in the few minutes left to her before sleep blotted out the misery of what had happened, she thought mostly about Mollie. Why hadn't Mollie just put the boot in? She could have made things ten times worse, and yet she was trying to make a deal: "You don't say nothing about my mum and dad – not to anyone – and I won't tell them about you're being here tonight." It sounded as though she'd meant it, too. Mind you, the deal was off, because Len and Mags now knew about the trip to the woods. But maybe Sam was right about Mollie. Maybe she was having a lousy life, just like everyone else. One thing seemed pretty certain – there wasn't a lot of love in the Mangles home.

Eventually, Gwynedd drifted into sleep.

CHAPTER 8

She was woken by Dave, wanting his breakfast. He tapped on her door, asking if she was ill. As she hauled herself out of bed, she saw the state of her sheets and pillow, streaked with smears of brown sauce and mushy peas. That meant a trip to the launderette or a back-breaking hour leaning over the bath. She groaned with dismay. Welcome to another wonderful day. And she'd have to get a move on if she was going to catch the school bus.

Dave stared at her. 'Well, where were you last night?'

'Nowhere. You go back to your telly. I'll get your breakfast.'

'You're in a state. What you been doing?'

'I went for a walk.'

'Where?'

'Out!' Her hands were shaking as she dropped spoonfuls of tea-leaves into the pot.

'You in trouble?'

She reckoned she could guess what he meant by trouble. 'Yeah,' she said. 'I'm pregnant. Going to have quads. Next week.' She poured boiling water from the kettle on to the tea-leaves. He was right. She was in a state. 'No, of course I'm not in trouble.'

'I'll know if you are.'

'Yeah. You'll be the last to know.'

She took him his tea in the front room, had a hot bath, and put on her school clothes. There wasn't any time for breakfast, and as she ran through the campsite and up to the car park, she searched her mind as to what she should do. Should she tell Sam about her raid on the camp? She wanted to tell him about the dead foxes, and make it real scary. But... suppose Sam asked why she'd gone in the first place? She'd have to say something about the Mangles, about her suspicions, and about her worries for Ben. And that would just about terrify Sam. She could tell him she just wanted to see where Mollie lived, but she wasn't sure how he'd take that. Whenever there was a row between her and Mollie, Sam seemed to take Mollie's side.

She didn't like that thought, and pushed it aside. No, the real point was that she couldn't say nothing to Sam about the Mangles' dogs, not with them adopting his precious Ben once they've moved into the cottage. So she had to keep the whole Mangles' business to herself. She was pretty sure that Mollie wouldn't say anything.

The school bus was pulling out as she sprinted into the car park. She skidded to a halt, right in front of it, forcing the driver to break sharply. He shook his fist at her, but let her on board, muttering something about 'an' I hope you've learned your lesson', as he crashed the bus into gear. Sam had expected big trouble between Gwynedd and Mollie on the bus, but to his surprise and relief, the journey to school was unusually quiet.

Gwynedd's entry into school was far more in character, bordering on the triumphal. Her old mates jostled each other for a chance to grab hold of her, shouting words of encouragement. Her enemies pushed and jeered as she passed. Sam watched the excitement go to her head. She marched across the playground, hands raised like a winning athlete doing a lap of honour. She punched the air. She was about to make a speech when her Year Tutor shoved his face in. By mid-morning she had been passed from Year Tutor to Head of Pastoral Care, to Deputy Head, and finally on to the Head. It wasn't the first time they had met.

'I shall be contacting your... er...' The Head rummaged through the papers from Gwynedd's file. What the hell was it? Parents or guardians?

'Dave,' said Gwynedd.

'...your grandad. I shall be contacting him today.'

'Oh yeah? And how you going to do that? On my mobile? It ain't charged. Bad luck.'

'By letter,' said the Head.

'Give it us an' I'll take it home this afternoon. Save you a stamp.'

'In the meantime, you will be suspended from school until I've spoken with your grandad... and...' There was more searching through papers. 'And I've contacted your social worker... Mrs...'

'Horseface,' said Gwynedd.

'...Horsfall. When you return to school... perhaps I should say *if* you return to school, I shall be watching you very closely.'

'That'll be nice,' said Gwynedd, 'Nice for you, that is. So... do I go home now? Yes? Right? Can you lend us the money for a minicab?'

'Your social worker will be here in ten minutes. In the meantime, you can wait in the corridor outside.' The Head tried to adopt an air that suggested she expected Gwynedd to do as she was told.

'Please yourself,' said Gwynedd. She left the room.

There was no chance to patch things up with Sam before Horseface arrived. The exit from school, with Gwynedd waving in triumph from the passenger seat of Horseface's Micra, was followed by a dismal ride back to the bungalow. Fortunately, Dave didn't wish to have his beloved T V interrupted, and after a brief and useless few words, Horseface departed.

That evening, she and Sam took Ben for a walk.

'You've got to get all this sorted out by next Thursday,' said Sam. 'You've got to be back at school by then.'

'Why?'

'Because that's when I'm supposed to be coming to stay with you.'

'So?'

'Mum won't let me if she knows you're in trouble.'

'Who says I'm in trouble? Anyway, how will Becky know? You won't tell her.'

'No.' Sam sighed. He could manage not to tell his mum so long as she didn't ask him. He'd lied to her before, from time to time, but that had been about small, personal things – whether he'd written a thank-you letter, done his homework, changed his underwear. This was big. The whole business of going to spend the night with Gwynedd was getting out of hand. One of the reasons why he wanted her back at school was so that he could keep an eye on her.

'That's all right then,' she said.

They walked on in silence for a while, then she said, 'Come on - what *do* you think of the Mangles?'

'Don't like 'em much,' he said. 'Mum's a bit worried about the way Len's trying to get her to lower the price of the cottage... but we're moving anyway. Not sure about them having Ben. I suppose he'll be all right with them.' He glanced across at her and was surprised to see worry on her face. 'Why? What do *you* think of them?'

'Me? Oh, I just... I just don't like them.'

He was surprised by the flatness of her voice. He had expected a bright and breezy condemnation of the Mangles. 'It can't be much fun for Mollie,' he said, 'having them for parents. We're both better off than she is.'

'Why'd you say that?'

'Would you fancy going home to the Mangles every day? Even if they are mad on dogs. Mollie's mum's bad enough. But what about having Len for a dad?'

Though Gwynedd longed to blurt out the red hot

secret about Len Mangle not being Mollie's real dad, she knew she had to hold her tongue. She was in possession of two secrets - the one about Len and the other about the dogs - and right now she couldn't divulge either. Not yet. 'Come on, race you to the gate.'

Sam spent most of the weekend pretending that he was listening to everything his mum said about what he was and was not to do while she was away.

'I'll be back next Saturday afternoon,' she said.

'Saturday?'

'I told you. I'm going for two nights.'

He pretended to remember.

Gwynedd spent the weekend rowing with Dave.

'Why should I have to go all the way to your bloody school just because you can't behave yourself?'

'Because you'd be the first to complain if you had me stuck under this roof with you all day, every day. And the school won't take me back unless you and Horseface go up there and vouch for me.'

'Vouch? What the bloody hell's "vouch"?'

'Go up there and promise them I'll be good.'

'Why can't you promise?'

'Because they wouldn't believe me.'

'Don't blame them.'

He wasn't going to be any help. She'd have to make all the effort.

'Let's have that bloody telly off for a start.' She stomped across the room, switched the set off and sat in the old armchair, the one her dad used to sit in.

'Look,' she said. 'Just come up to school for my sake. I'll cook you chips every night for a week if you'll just come up to school.' She was desperate to get back to normal as soon as possible, so there'd be less chance of a string of rows with him. Things had to be settled before Sam's officially uninvited arrival on Thursday night.

'You don't have to resort to bribery,' he said. 'I'm your grandad. I'll come up to the school and give that driver a piece of my mind.'

She regretted passing on so many details of the fight on the bus, but was strangely touched. She couldn't remember the last time he'd referred to himself as her grandad.

'And let's have a rest from chips for a while,' he said. 'Something healthy instead. Salad... bit of fish... grilled...'

'You all right?' she said.

He made a face. 'Course I'm all right. Don't fuss. Just get some salad for tea.'

They made the journey to Llandrindod on Tuesday morning in Grace Horsfall's car.

Dave sat in the front with the social worker; Gwynedd sulked in the back. Grace Horsfall was keen to make the most of a rare chance to talk to the guardian of one of her most difficult cases.

'How are you, Mr Hughes?' she said. 'How's your health? How are you and Gwynedd getting on? Being a single grandparent must be even harder than being a single parent. How are you *managing*?'

87

'He's fine,' said Gwynedd.

'Good!' The social worker glanced at Dave, sitting next to her. She leant over and lowered her voice. 'You know if... er, if... well, if it *did* become too much for you, there are ways in which we can help...'

'What'd she say?'

Dave twisted in his seat to face Gwynedd. 'She said you'd better not give me any trouble or she'll have you put in a home. And before you get your fists up, have a think about that, because I'm certainly going to.'

Gwynedd spent the rest of the journey fighting back the desire to punch them both. At school, the discussion with the Year Head and Deputy Head was swift and business-like. Gwynedd would be allowed to return to school if she apologised to the bus driver, and gave a written undertaking that her behaviour would be better in future. She promised she would make the apology, and wrote the undertaking there and then, offering to seal it with her blood.

'None of your stupid jokes,' said Dave. The Deputy Head looked relieved. He thought she had meant it.

'Well,' said the Deputy Head, 'in view of this, I think we can say that the school will insist on no more than a three day suspension.'

Gwynedd did a rapid calculation. 'Good,' she said. 'I'll be back in a couple of hours.' She looked at their blank faces. 'I didn't come in Thursday – that's one day. I came in Friday, but you sent me home two hours later. I didn't come in yesterday. So that's three days, all but two hours.' She looked at the clock. 'I can start back at twelve. Hardly worth waiting, is it?'

The Year Head was not without a sense of humour. 'A three day suspension does need confirmation by the governors,' he said to the Deputy. 'And Gwynedd does have a point.'

'Good,' said Gwynedd again. 'Tell you what, we'll say nothing about the assault, an' I'll just start straight away and be extra good for a couple of hours. Saves me hanging about and getting into mischief.'

She got her way, and managed to hold herself in check for the whole of that day and the next. When Thursday morning came, she arrived at the Harpers' cottage bright and early, in time to witness Sam and Becky's parting.

'You've packed your toothbrush and toothpaste?'

'Yeah.'

'And pyjamas?... sweater?... I don't know how cold that bungalow gets at night... I'm just a bit worried about how you'll get in touch with me if anything goes wrong. There's no phone at that bungalow.'

'I've got my mobile.'

'Make sure it's charged and you're in credit. Do you need money?...' Her parental concern was interrupted by the arrival of Gwynedd. 'Oh, hi, Gwynedd. Is everything all right?'

'Grand. Don't you worry about Sam. I'll look after him.'

'It's very kind of your grandfather to invite him.'

'That's what I think,' said Gwynedd, and she beamed at Sam. 'He's so looking forward to it.' They could take that how they liked. "He" could be Dave or Sam. It didn't have to be a lie.

'...clean pants and socks for Friday...'

'I can change when I come back to feed Ben tomorrow morning,' said Sam. This was revolting – like being undressed in public. But he noted the look on mum's face. 'Yeah, yeah. Clean socks and pants and dinner jacket and knickerbockers and...'

'...flannel...' said Becky.

'Mum, we'll miss the bus. Have a good time in Bristol. See you later, Ben.'

The dog wagged his tail delightedly. Someone had mentioned his name.

Sam grabbed his bag. 'Let's go.' He dashed off.

'...dinner money!' shouted Becky, and she held it out in her hand.

Sam skidded to a halt and ran back. 'Thanks, mum,' he said as he snatched it out of her hand.

'And don't forget your homework tonight!' Some hope, she thought.

'Don't worry, Becky. I'll make sure he does it.' Some hope, thought Gwynedd.

CHAPTER 9

Gwynedd was determined that Thursday night was going to be a tremendous success. She cooked Dave a special tea - bit of steak with onions, served with the salad that he now insisted on having every day.

'How about a beer with that?'

'No. Thanks, Gwynedd. That'll do fine for me. Got any fruit for afters?'

Fruit? Dave must be totally losing it...

When he'd finished his tea, she took the tray back to the kitchen. The washing-up could wait – more fun to do it with Sam. She changed quickly into jeans and an orange zip-up top, put on her old trainers, and rushed out.

She jogged down the lane, her mind fizzing as she checked that all was ready for Sam's visit. He'd have to sleep on the couch, but she'd got clean sheets for him, and an old blanket from the cupboard that she had secretly aired at the weekend, and then shoved back in the cupboard on Sunday night. He could have one of her pillows, and she'd put a sweet on it like they did on the TV when a couple went to stay at a posh hotel… a toffee – she'd managed to pinch a fistful from a shop in Llandrindod at midday break.

She reached the cottage and thumped on the door. 'Come on, Beast,' she shouted. 'Beauty's here!'

He made a snuffling noise as he opened the door. 'Oh,' he said, with mock disappointment. 'Poor Beast hoped it really was Beauty, but it's you.'

She hit him and gave him a hug.

They took Ben for his usual evening run. The sun's rays still streaked the eastern side of the valley. They scrambled up the short grass, dodging between the outcrops of rock and trying to keep up with the racing dog. The air was cooling rapidly, but the effort needed for the climb kept them warm. Halfway up, they sat on the hillside and gazed down into the valley. There was Sam's cottage, half hidden by the trees that grew along the stream. And there was Gwynedd's bungalow away to the left, and their old Junior school on the edge of the town. From deep within the woods to the north, a wisp of blue smoke curled upwards.

'That's the Mangles,' she said. 'Cooking their tea… rat kebab.'

'What must it be like for poor Mollie?' he said.

'Why do you keep saying "poor" Mollie?'

'Len's a cheat, and Mags is weird. Keeps going on about only having one kid – like there's something wrong. We haven't got any brothers or sisters, but there's nothing wrong with us, is there?'

'Not with *me*,' said Gwynedd. 'Maybe there's

92

something wrong with her. Maybe she wants to adopt you. Maybe she fancies you.'

'You're always going on about people fancying people.'

'Well, they do.'

'But you say it all the time. You never talk about important things.'

She thought about the fright she had had on her visit to the camp in the woods, and about Ben and the Mangles. 'You wouldn't like it if I did.'

'It'd make a change.' He got up and ran off to play with Ben.

She was hurt by his words. As Vinnie said, life came, and there was nothing you could do about it. Suppose she did tell Sam about how she reckoned there might be a bad time ahead for Ben with the Mangles? Sam would go to pieces. But bloomin' Ben was only a dog, and not even a working dog.

It was getting cold, time to go. She stood up. There was Sam calling to his bloody dog, stroking it, and talking to it like it was a baby. This was getting to be a mess, just like everything in life.

'Race you back to the cottage.' She hurtled down the hillside, reaching the stream long before Sam, who kept stopping to throw the ball for Ben. As she crossed the trickling water by the stepping stones, some mischief within tempted her to reach down, remove the last stepping stone, and chuck it downstream. She sprang lightly on to the bank, ducked behind a clump of hazel, and waited, hoping that her orange top wouldn't give her away. A moment later, she heard Sam and Ben approach. The dog plunged into the stream. Sam came steadily on, stepping from stone to stone, knowing the route so well that he didn't bother to look where he was going.

She heard a single splash and a most un-Harper like cuss. She felt suddenly mean, and was about to rush over to comfort him and apologise, when a door slammed behind her. She whirled round. It must have been the back door of the cottage.

'Sam!' she shouted, but he took no notice. 'Sam!'

The light had almost gone from the sky, and the back of the cottage was screened by a trellis of honeysuckle, but she made out a figure vanishing round the corner by the water butt, into the side passage that led to the lane. She sprinted up the garden. She heard the gate click open, and shoes scrunch on loose chippings at the side of the lane. This was someone quick and light on his feet. By the time she reached the lane, there was no one in sight. A wet and panting Ben joined her.

'Who was it, Ben? Go on, boy. Track 'em down.'

But Ben wasn't a tracker. The dog wagged its tail, gazed happily at her and then shook itself vigorously. Droplets of water flew through the air.

'Brainless, useless animal!' She ran back down the passage and into the garden.

Sam was sitting on the grass, ripping off his trainers and peeling off his soaking socks. He had done what she wanted, assumed the final stone was in its rightful place, and stumbled into the stream, plunging his feet into the cold water. He flung Ben's ball into the flower bed and looked angrily up at Gwynedd.

'You did that, didn't you.'

'There's no harm done.'

'Oh, really? Look at my Nikes.'

'Bloody Nikes! Bit of good Welsh water won't hurt. But listen, someone's been in your cottage. He come out and legged it down the passage. I saw him.'

Sam stood up – one shoe off and one shoe on.

'Diddle, diddle dumpling,' she said.

'Piss off!'

She hadn't meant it unkindly, and was hurt again. 'And you! And your Nikes.' She turned away. 'I'm going to see what he was up to. Make sure nothing's been pinched.'

They went to the back door. It was shut. There were no signs of damage to it.

'He didn't break in, then,' said Gwynedd. 'Sure you locked it when we took Ben out?' She looked at Sam. 'You didn't, did you?'

'Of course I did.'

'Liar.'

'Takes one to know one,' said Sam.

'Yeah, but I know *how* to lie. You're a right weed at lying. You gotta lie quick. No good goin' puce in the face with trying to think of something to say.'

'Why don't you just shut up.'

'Come on,' she said. She opened the door and peered in. Sam's school bag was on the kitchen table, as he had left it… except… it had been opened. Books, pens and paper were scattered in a heap. And the intruder had helped himself to a packet of biscuits.

'He might not be alone, there may be another one upstairs,' whispered Gwynedd. 'We'd better go quietly.'

Their silent entrance was ruined by Ben, who bounded in, claws rattling over the tiled floor, which the dog sniffed noisily.

'He's hopeless,' said Gwynedd.

'He's doing his best.'

'Too late now. See what's been pinched.'

Sam checked his bag. To him, the only thing that mattered was his mobile. It was safe, still zipped in the side pocket where he'd left it. There were three unanswered text messages on it, all from his mother. The first was fine. The second was agitated. The third was rattled.

They stamped noisily upstairs. Sam went to check his room, Gwynedd went into Becky's. It was very clean, very tidy. The bed was made. The carpet was spotless. Everything was where it was supposed to be – clothes in the wardrobe, undies and bras in the drawers, shoes in large plastic wallets hanging from the back of the door. The dressing table was neatly arranged – box of tissues here, comb and brush there (with no old hairs in either), cotton wool, smellies, creams and lotions. She'll have taken all her best stuff with her, thought Gwynedd, to seduce this Martin, not that he'll need much seducing. She wondered what it would be like, to live in a house with another woman in it, to discuss fashion and feelings. Then she shrugged her shoulders.

What you've never had, you never miss.

Sam came in. 'It's OK. Nothing's missing.' He stared at Gwynedd, sitting at his mother's dressing table. 'What are you doing?'

'Nothing,' she said, getting up. 'Lucky escape, then… leaving the back door open.'

'I didn't leave it open.'

'As good as.'

'Oh, do piss off! You're getting on my nerves.' Sam wasn't looking forward to phoning his mum. If only Gwynedd would shut up and clear off. He didn't want her around when he phoned.

'Don't you want to catch whoever broke in? You've got your posh mobile. Dial 999.'

'You don't dial on a mobile. You punch the number in.' his voice was laced with sarcasm.

'I know something I'd like to punch in.' A part of her wanted to laugh.

'Don't keep going on and on.'

'I'm not going on and on. I'm going home. Coming?'

'No. I'm staying here… with Ben.'

'You stay with your smelly old dog, then.'

'And you go back to your mad old grandad.'

That did it! Him and his bloody ma and his bloody belongings and all this going to Bristol and his stupid bloody dog… She bit her lip, pushed him aside, thumped down the stairs, and left – slamming the door.

Sam followed her slowly down the stairs. Ben was still sniffing round the kitchen. 'She's a pig,' he said. Ben scratched the back door and whimpered. 'Oh, shut up!' This was a fine time for the dog to act miserable.

It was getting late. Time for Ben to have his feed. Sam took a tin of dog food from the cupboard and the tin opener from the drawer. He opened the tin and scooped large chunks of meat into Ben's bowl. The dog wolfed it down.

His mobile rang. It was Becky. She was worried. She'd texted three times – he knew. He hadn't answered – he knew. She was worried – he guessed. Was everything all right? – he lied. And how was Gwynedd? – he lied again. Where was he? – and again… She wanted to speak to Dave – he invented a reason why she couldn't, telling his mum that Gwynedd's granddad was watching television. Half a mile away, it was true, though Sam didn't know it. Becky told him to phone her first thing in the morning – he promised. She told him she loved him. He said 'yes', in a husky voice. She asked if he'd done his homework. He said he had got it in front of him now – it was a relief to be able to include some truth in this clumsy conversation. She said 'goodnight' – he repeated the word, and switched off the phone.

He felt lonely, and turned to Ben. 'Time to go out,' he said. He opened the back door. 'Go on. Out!'

The dog wouldn't move. 'Out! There's nothing to be frightened of.' All the same… Gwynedd wouldn't have made up that story about someone running out of the house. Well, she might. In which case, it was a lousy trick. So… good riddance to her. He was glad he wasn't going to stay with her and Dave, though he wished he hadn't called her grandad "mad". Never mind, a night on his own in the cottage would be good. He'd log on, and have an extended session in the chat room with some of the lads.

But, for some reason, he didn't want to go up to his room. It just felt that bit safer downstairs. Just in case. If he had to leg it, better to be near the front door. He locked the back door, and then sat in the front room, sensing the darkness outside getting deeper and deeper. Not full of ogres or aliens or phantoms or witches or anything that Little Huwie went on about – just a kind of evil sort of soup.

He told himself this was ridiculous. It was just an empty cottage. What harm could there be in anything *empty*? There weren't any skeletons in the cupboards or aliens in the light sockets. There weren't any homicidal maniacs with long thin-bladed knives, stealing from room to room, sneaking up behind him, ready to slip the knife under his ribs or to stab it deep in his throat. His hands reached up to his throat and then down to his ribs, just to make sure that all was well, and his body twisted round to check nothing was behind him. He tried not to imagine the intruder returning. He tried television, food, and even homework. He collected all the old newspapers and rubbish he could find and burnt them in the grate. But then he feared the flickering flames might attract unwelcome attention. He reminded himself he wasn't a kid any more, that he was heading for the big city, where the drug pushers and gangs ruled, and where you survived by being cool. Or perished.

For some reason, it didn't help that Ben was doing his entire "Watch me, love me" routine, parading round with his feeding bowl in his mouth while uttering strangulated growls. Nothing helped. Nothing brought the place to life.

The ash from the last of the burning newspapers whispered in the grate, and Sam felt cold. He told himself that he wasn't cold, but it didn't work. This was hopeless, shameful, pathetic. He wasn't even alone. There was Ben. Useless, stupid Ben, who wouldn't even go out in the garden for some stupid useless reason.

Two minutes later, Sam dropped a pile of dog biscuits on the kitchen floor, snatched up his bag and ran from the cottage. Six minutes later, he was banging on the door of Gwynedd's bungalow.

She let him in immediately. 'Oh, Sam,' she said. 'I'm so glad you've come.'

CHAPTER 10

Dave was in a bad mood. There was no warm welcome for Sam.

'Don't like you as much as her other boyfriend,' he said.

'It's very kind of you to invite me,' said Sam. What the hell was the old man on about?

'I never bloody invited you. She did. And you both got a bloody nerve.'

Eventually Dave shuffled off to bed, complaining that his own parlour had been turned into a doss-house. Sam breathed a sigh of relief, and yawned. Today had become one of those days when he felt he'd never forgive his father for dying. And here was Gwynedd hovering over him like a red kite.

'Can I go to bed now?'

'When I've given you a goodnight kiss,' she said.

Gwynedd slept well, woke early. It was just six o'clock when she thumped ferociously on the front room door. 'I hope you're decent,' she shouted. 'Cos I'm coming in anyway.' She flung the door open. Sam cowered beneath the thin sheet and smelly blanket. She threatened to yank the bedding from him.

'Do you need help getting dressed?'

'Get off!'

'Get up! I've got to have this room cleared of all trace of you by half seven, so's I can give Dave his breakfast. And you said you wanted to take your barmy dog for a walk before school.'

He groaned. 'What sort of hotel is this? I woke up with a toffee in my ear, now I'm kicked out of bed. All right. Ready in five minutes. Now, get out!'

They walked down to the cottage. Sam fitted the key in the lock and opened the front door. 'I'm not going to tell mum about the break-in... That's odd. Where's Ben?'

They found the dog in the kitchen, trembling in his basket. As soon as he saw Sam, he gave a half-hearted bark and hurried to him, but the dog didn't leap up, and he didn't do his usual trick of gripping Sam's arm in his jaws.

'What's the matter, Ben?'

'He's just not used to being alone. He missed you,' said Gwynedd. 'Like he'll miss you when you go to Bristol. He won't be the only one. Have to get used to it though, won't we, Ben.'

Sam wasn't listening. He opened the back door, but the dog wouldn't leave the kitchen. 'Go on, Ben. Out! You know the rule. No breakfast till you've been out.'

He went outside and called the dog from the garden. 'Come on, Ben! Come *on*!'

Gwynedd stopped nosing through the kitchen cupboards, and went out to join him. He pointed to the small patch of grass in the centre of the garden. Strewn across it were the remains of the ball that he had hurled into the flower bed after his footbath in the stream.

'You didn't do that, did you?' he said.

'Course not - not after it's been in your rotten dog's mouth.' She picked up one of the pieces. 'Something with long, sharp teeth done that. Fox, most likely.' She thought of the rotting bodies in the woods.

'You reckon foxes did that, too?' Sam pointed to a clump of delphiniums that had been trampled into the earth. 'And that... and that?' There were broken plants everywhere in the garden and other signs of a nocturnal invasion – overturned flower pots, savaged beansticks, and a chewed length of garden hose.

'My mum'll have a fit. If it was foxes, maybe they came up through the trees. By the stream.'

They went down to the stream together. Ben had crept out on to the small patio, but there he stayed. At the edge of the water, not far from where Gwynedd had removed the last stepping stone, there were clear prints in the moist mud.

'Those don't look like foxes' prints to me.'

'Just shut up about foxes. We ain't gonna find out what it was, no more than we're gonna find out who was in the cottage last night. And whoever it was and whatever it was ain't here now, so it don't matter. I'm going. It's time to get Dave's breakfast.'

She moved away, then heard him call after her to wait while he put some biscuits down for Ben. To wait, or not to wait? What did it matter? Sam was going to Bristol. Dave wanted to put her in a home. Life was all downhill, whichever way you looked at it.

Life came and went. Sam was taken away from her for 48 whole hours. Becky lugged him off to Bristol, to show him off to the school she'd chosen for him. Gwynedd didn't get much fun out of the two days. She didn't enjoy the lonely trudge through the playground and up to the car park. She hadn't the heart to hang around the swings practising gymnastics, so she always arrived at the car park long before the school bus was ready to go. She couldn't even summon up the energy to spar with Mollie. She stood in the lunchtime queue for chips, less than half her attention on Vinnie and his plans for the future.

'...you know what I mean?'

'No,' she said. 'I don't. I ain't been listening. Sorry, Vinnie.'

'Brilliant. I was saying, this bike I'm gonna get – the Birmingham B – you can get it with what they call a pillion seat. It's optional, like, see? So... if you wanted to *mount up* behind me... like Clint Eastwood always has... or *had*, I should say, a woman *mounts up* behind him... we could go somewhere together. Like, if you wanted that, I'd get the optional. But if you didn't fancy it, I don't think I'd bother.' Vinnie was not overloaded with mates.

On the second evening, while Sam was still in Bristol, she went into town to do the shopping. She could think of nothing to do but shuffle round the supermarket, and as she did so, a head of angry steam built up inside her. Bloody Sam! He hadn't called. He hadn't texted. She was used to being let down, but she had never expected it from Sam.

Right on cue, her mobile rang. She fished it from her pocket, hoping it was Sam, and immediately ready and willing to forgive him. But it was Vinnie, texting, wanting to meet – "…20 SX. TND FJ." She peered along the supermarket aisles. Sure enough, there he was, by a stack of tinned sardines, waving like an idiot.

She waved back. So he'd been following her, watching her. Well, maybe there was more to him… He asked if she fancied a walk, offered to carry her shopping home. They passed through the checkout and walked down to the river. Vinnie carried the shopping in one hand, and slipped his other arm round her. He had had his hair cut. Where once all had been long and lanky, there was now a close-cropped dome.

He steered her towards the rocks where she and Sam had sat and talked so often.

'I got plenty of time. Let's sit and have a chat, eh?' They sat. 'And I got a present for you.' He handed her a creased envelope, sealed, with her name written on it, and the words "WITH LOVE". From the feel of it, she thought it might be a flower, or a roll of tobacco, or something made of string. She opened the envelope and took out a small coil of hair.

'It's a bracelet.'

'This is your hair?'

'I got the idea from Clint Eastwood, in *The Outlaw Josey Wales*. All the best ideas come from Wales, know what I mean?'

It was one of his rare jokes and it made her smile. Tell the truth, he didn't look so bad with his hair cut. You could do worse than Vinnie…

'Put it on,' he said.

'I don't reckon it'll fit.'

'Force it. Give it over here.' He took hold of her arm and tried to roll the ring of hair over her hand. It stuck. He tried harder.

'It's no good. And that hurts.'

'Bit of soap might do it. Or shampoo.' It was another joke. 'I told Mollie it'd be too small.'

'Mollie made it?'

'I said you got strong wrists. Big hands, too.' Vinnie gave up the struggle. 'I got more hair at home. I'll get Mollie to make it bigger.'

'No, it's OK. I'll keep it anyway.' She crammed the hair back in the envelope and stuffed it in her pocket.

'Wear it on a chain round your neck. Unless it'll make your boobs itch.'

'If it does, you won't be scratching them.'

'Yeah.' He looked at her in what was meant to be a tender way. 'We get on really well, don't we,' he said. He hadn't expected the gift to be such a success. 'Mollie doesn't like you. Mind you, I don't believe what she says about you and Sam that time he stayed at your bungalow. Sam's not the sort.' He laughed. 'Mollie swears Sam's saving his whatsit for their wedding night. But I think he's just a nerd, know what I mean.'

Vinnie had both hands free. He put one on her shoulder, and with the other, turned her face towards him. She knew what was coming. He kissed her, not roughly, but the kiss had no tenderness in it. Gwynedd had been kissed before, but she had never returned a kiss. Now, she kissed him back, making it as gentle as she could – not with an open mouth, but softly, letting her lips roll a little on his. His response was to try to stick his tongue in her mouth, and to begin pawing and scrabbling at her breasts. She wondered if he had got the idea from a book, or off the Internet, or from one of Clint Eastwood's bloody films.

She pulled away, and said woodenly, 'No, Vinnie.'

'Am I doing it wrong?' He wiped his mouth on his sleeve.

'How should I know?' said Gwynedd.

'I thought you must have, like, done it with blokes.'

'Why?'

'Because you're a girl, and you get mad with people, and you're a bit wild, and the teachers don't like you, and, being black, like, and...'

'And what?'

'And because you're not like the others.'

She didn't lose her temper. 'You need to think about things a bit more, Vinnie,' she said.

107

'I bin thinking about this a lot,' he said.

'Were you thinking about me?'

'Yur. You bet.' A sly grin spread across his face.

'I mean *really* thinking about me. About how I'd feel. Putting yourself in my shoes.'

'Like a transvestite.'

She stared at the river.

He kept trying to fondle her. She pushed him off each time. After a while, he said, 'Is that it? Bloomin' heck.' He got up from the rock, swung a kick at her shopping bags, and left.

'Oh, Sam,' she said.

She picked up the shopping, and made her way back to the bungalow. She cooked Dave's tea – a bit of fish and some broccoli, followed by raspberries from the garden. Dave had picked the raspberries between races on the TV, but he hadn't bothered to get rid of the mouldy ones or the little maggots that waved their heads at her from the sinkful of water she washed them in. She remembered other, bigger maggots in the fox carcases, and shuddered. As she prodded the broccoli to check whether it was ready, and flipped the fish under the grill, she thought about Vinnie and Sam, comparing the two, wishing she liked Vinnie more and Sam less. She sank so deep in thought, she overcooked the fish, and then discovered that the over-soaked raspberries had turned to mush in the sink.

Dave made the fuss she expected when she took him his tea, but she put so little energy into answering him back that he asked if she was ill. That made her feel tearful, and she hurried back to the kitchen. Do the washing-up. Take your mind off things. She slid the plates and cutlery into the hot sudsy water, plunged her hands in, and then the tears came. She leaned against the old sink unit, while the tears slipped down her cheeks and into the foam. She swore at herself, telling herself it was her life and she better bloody get on with it. She tried to bribe herself into cheerfulness by taking a brand new scourer from the cupboard, to tackle the grease on the grill pan. It was a rare treat that got the pan reasonably clean, but did nothing for her spirits.

Company. She needed company or she'd go mad, banged up on your own here with Dave. Get out. Go up into town, to the chippie. See if Vinnie's around, the Paki lad, anyone. She dried her hands and went to the bedroom, to change out of her school clothes. It was a warm enough evening for a T shirt on top – the pale blue one would do. She rejected jeans and trousers. For once, she would wear a skirt. The denim mini. Thick tights, pair of black trainers, the earrings, and she was ready. She forced her spirits to rise. Then she remembered she had to feed Ben, and was supposed to let him have a run. Well, she'd do that first and then head for town.

She got only as far as the Harper cottage. The door was open. Maybe Becky and Sam were back a day early. Good. She stepped inside and called. 'Sam! Are you there? Becky?'

The figure that blocked the dark narrow hallway

was too big to be either. It was a man, but she couldn't see his face. Something was wrong. Why wasn't Ben barking? For just a second or two she was frightened. The intruder moved towards her. His face came into the light. It was Len Mangles.

'Not here, dear,' he said.

'Who is it, Len?' That was Mags, calling from upstairs.

'It's the child, Magsie. The one that's always hanging around.'

Child? Bloody nerve! Gwynedd got over her fears. 'What are you doing here?'

'Are you simple-minded, dear? I thought you'd been told. We're buying the place.'

'How did you get in?'

'Not that it's any of your business but we got the keys from the agent. And that lovely Mrs Harper knows all about it. Satisfied?'

Mags came downstairs. Her narrow eyes looked Gwynedd up and down in a disapproving examination. 'What's this then, Len? *Another* party?'

'Where's Ben?'

'The dog's eating in the kitchen. The cat's dead – curiosity killed it. There's a moral there.'

'Now then, Len. Manners.' Mags spoke with her cigarette clamped firmly between her thin lips. 'You'll have to forgive him, Little Miss… what's your name?'

'That's for you to find out,' said Gwynedd.

'Charming,' said Mags.

'It's Gwynedd, isn't it,' said Len. 'Lovely name. Like

it came out of a poem or something. Well now, Miss Gwynedd, we're just making plans for when this adorable love nest is ours...'

'And the dog,' said Mags.

'Oh, yes, *and* the dog. I'm potty about that animal. Love him like he was my own child, I do.'

Just for a moment, Gwynedd felt suddenly sorry for Mollie.

Len leered at Gwynedd. 'Sorry to have to say that, dear, you being a child yourself. Kids, eh? A blessing when they're young, a blessing when you're old.'

'That'll be the day.' The woman gave birth to a monosyllabic grunt that may have been a laugh.

It didn't take a genius to realise that the Mangles were deliberately blocking the hall so that she couldn't get in, but Gwynedd stood her ground. 'I've come to take Ben for his run.'

'All done, dear,' said Len. 'Mags had a bit of a frolic with him earlier. We're about ready for off ourselves.'

'Off to your dump in the woods.' The moment she'd uttered the words, Gwynedd wished she hadn't.

Len looked her up and down, and smiled maliciously. 'Yes,' he said. 'Our "dump" in the woods. Where we found you the other night, shoving your pretty face where it'll never be wanted. Understand? Never!'

Gwynedd was frightened now. 'Yeah, OK,' she said, hurriedly. 'I understand.'

'I wonder...' But at that moment his mobile rang. He flipped it open and peered at it.

'I'll have to take this one, Mags.' He pushed Gwynedd

away from the cottage, ahead of him. 'You'll excuse me, I know. The signal's none too strong at our "dump" as you so rudely call it, so we have to take calls when we can.' He stopped by the gate. 'Magsie, perhaps you'll see this young lady off the premises...'

'I shan't prolong the party,' said Mags. 'Hop it.' She took the cigarette out of her mouth for just long enough to sneer at Gwynedd.

But Gwynedd was determined to have the last taunt. 'How's your Mollie?'

Mags took the cigarette out of her mouth. 'Never mind Mollie,' she said. 'You keep her out of this. She don't want you for a friend no more than we want you for a neighbour. Hop it.'

Gwynedd walked briskly away, her mind working fast. She'd make a quick circuit of the cottage and come back via the wood and the stream, to creep up the side of the building and hopefully eavesdrop on Len's conversation. She didn't trust the Mangles, or believe their story about the agent, the keys and Becky. Like Sam had said, 'it takes a liar to know a liar', and she knew that Len Mangles was lying.

She climbed the gate into the field that bordered the cottage garden, and, using the hedge as cover, ran down to the wood. Keeping to the Harpers' side of the stream, she made her way up the garden, behind the line of shrubs and trees. It took her less than a minute to reach the passage at the side of the cottage. Here there was somewhere to hide, right by the corner. She squeezed between the wall and the water-butt.

It was all for nothing. She could hear Len, only a few metres away, but couldn't distinguish what he was saying. The conversation came to an end. She heard the single word "*adios*", then the click as he snapped his mobile shut. He called out to Mags.

'It's on for Friday... half past...'

There was no answer from Mags, and Len went into the cottage, shutting the door behind him. Now was the time for Gwynedd to make her getaway. She counted to ten to make sure it was safe, and turned to head back down the passage and return to the road the way she had come. It didn't work.

The passage, like the hall before, was blocked, this time by Mags.

'You don't do as you're told,' said Mags. 'That's bad.'

'You got no right to tell me what to do. This ain't your cottage...'

'Not yet,' said Mags. 'But it very soon will be, and when it is... don't think you can walk in whenever you like. Imagine if Len or me mistook you for a trespasser or a thief, and set the dog on you... if you get my drift.'

'Because that dog won't be little Bennikins here...' Len had come out of the cottage by the front door.

Gwynedd was trapped between the two Mangles. She could see Ben cowering behind Len. She called to the dog. Ben began to move towards her, tail wagging, but slowly. Len called the dog back. It halted, ears drooping, tail down, and haunches trembling.

'Good boy, Ben,' said Len, but he never took his eyes off Gwynedd.

She called Ben to her again. The dog didn't move.

'He don't seem to want to come to you, dear, does he?' said Len. 'I really think you should go now, and leave him. He might get confused otherwise, and like the rest of us, dogs need a lot of correction when they're confused. You ought to think about that, dear. There's a good little lesson there for you...'

CHAPTER 11

Dave woke her up. 'Not going to see the Harpers off then?'

Gwynedd had overslept, and on this of all days, the day that Sam was leaving Wales and moving to Bristol. She had no idea what the time was. She ran all the way down to the cottage and discovered she was too late. The removals men were loading up the contents of the Harper cottage. Becky and Sam were still there, but parked in the lane was the black SUV. And, while Len was chatting amiably to Becky Harper, he was already fondling the dog that had become the cause of so much fear and woe.

Gwynedd hid from sight. Even when the taxi arrived to take Sam and Becky away, she didn't dare show herself, in case Len or Mags saw her. There were tears in her eyes when she turned to climb slowly back up the hill to the bungalow.

Weeks passed. The holidays ended. The long, boring autumn term began, always the worst in the year as far as Gwynedd was concerned. The camp site emptied, the tourists drove away. Dave gave up smoking, which made his cough and his temper worse than ever, so he took up smoking again. He and Gwynedd rowed all the time – about the state of the bungalow, about her lack of respect, about the food she gave him. He complained that she was trying to starve him to death with a diet of "green water", though he'd originally been the one who insisted on salads and fruit and daily bloody broccoli.

'Going to the bathroom all night,' he moaned.

When Gwynedd retaliated by cooking him an old-style fry-up, he accused her of trying to kill him by giving him a heart attack. It was all nonsense. They were simply two unhappy people imprisoned together in a brick bungalow on the edge of the Welsh mountains.

She phoned Sam, even wrote him a letter, only the second she'd written in her life. The first had been to her ma five years ago – a pathetic, plaintive note that never got a reply, because it had never been posted. She'd thrown it in the living room fire. The letter to Sam did at least get a stamp and a hopeful kiss just before she slipped it into the post-box by the car park in Rhayader.

Overnight, her bit of paper to Sam crossed with a bit of paper from him to her. It was waiting for her when she came home from school one Friday afternoon – a little early, at the school's request. She took it to her room, tore it open, and read it. He wanted to come and spend some of half term with her. He missed Wales. He missed the mountains. He missed the red kites –

Bristol was full of dirty pigeons and noisy seagulls. He missed Ben. He missed her.

That night, she gave Dave the best tea he'd had for weeks.

Over the next few days, she and Sam made the arrangements. She would meet him at the station in Llandrindod Wells off an afternoon train on the Wednesday of half term. They would get on the bus to Rhayader and walk down to the river just like they used to in the old days. Gwynedd took great care of the text Sam sent saying he was really "XI-TD" about coming. She could hardly wait.

Half term arrived. Gwynedd spent much of the first four days doing sums in her head. How long would it be until Sam arrived? Ninety-six hours... seventy-two hours... forty-eight hours... twenty-four hours...

On the Wednesday morning of half term, she woke before dawn and lay in bed until she heard Dave's alarm go off. Seven thirty. She had exactly nine hours and seven minutes before she met Sam at Llandrindod Wells station. He was probably already up and about, with Becky fussing over him, and desperate to get rid of him so's she could have a couple of days with her Fancy Martin. It would be a long journey for Sam – Bristol to Swansea, and then the Welsh crawler out to Llanelli and up the valleys. But on the last leg, from Llandrindod to Rhayader, he'd have company. She and Sam would be together like they used to be on the old school bus.

She dressed quickly, not bothering to wash. It was the usual mid October half-term outfit – sweater, trousers, trainers. She went into the kitchen to prepare Dave's breakfast. As with the ciggies, he'd gone back to fry-ups but no longer dipped his bread in the bacon fat.

He popped his head round the door while she was cooking.

'You all right?' she said.

'Why shouldn't I be?'

'Search me. You got everything you want with me slaving away and you not lifting a finger.'

'You watch your tongue.'

'You watch it,' she said, and stuck it out for him to admire. He went back to the front room.

She wondered what was going on in his daft head. He'd as good as given up arguing, but was giving her a lot of funny looks instead. Maybe he was plotting to have her put in a home. Maybe he had something on his chest beside nicotine tar and a load of... what was Sam's word? Muckus? No matter, he'd spit it out sooner or later, and when he did he'd get as good as he gave, stupid old beggar.

She plonked the plate on his tray and took it to him.

'Bon appetite,' she said.

'Don't be so bloody cheeky.'

But when she went back for his empty plate fifteen minutes later (only eight hours and twenty two minutes now till Sam's arrival), he told her to stay, ordered her to sit down. Here it comes, she thought... a moan, and it'll be a big one. He'd never told her to sit down before. She didn't obey the order.

'What's going on?' he said.

She wasn't falling for that. Teachers had been trying that on for years. You might catch Little Huwie with an opener like that. He'd blab his way into confessing half a dozen crimes: 'You mean the broken window? No? Then it must be the fight in the Girls Toilet... No? Oh, well then, the fire behind the bike shed...?' Dave would have to do much better than that if he hoped to get anything out of her.

'What makes you think anything's going on?' she said.

He said nothing. Right, she thought, two can play that game. Gwynedd folded her arms and clamped her mouth shut. Keep quiet for ten seconds and adults can't bear it. They have to say something. Ten seconds passed... fifteen... Gwynedd exploded. 'All right then. You and Horseface want me out of here and into some bloody kids home. Good! That's what I want too. Get away from you. Good bloody riddance! I'll go and pack now...'

'You stay where you are.'

She got up and made for the door.

'For weeks and weeks something's been wrong.' He spoke slowly, and quietly. 'You haven't been yourself. Not since that night back in July when you went out late. And when you come back... God knows what time... you was crying. Sobbing. I looked in on you later, two in the morning it was, and you was trembling in your bed. So what was that all about?'

She sat down. If he makes me cry, she thought, I'll hit him.

'Is it that young man that keeps hanging about?'

It took a breath or two before she realised he was talking about Vinnie. 'No, course not.'

'No "course not" about it. Plenty of girls your age, and younger, get into trouble.'

Thank God! He wasn't going to make her cry. He was going to make her laugh. Get into trouble with Vinnie! Not bloomin' likely. 'I'm not having a baby, if that's what you mean.'

'I'm not a fool, Gwynedd, any more than you are. I see what's going on, and I see a young girl, who's usually got more fight and spirit in her than the Welsh front row, shuffling round this bloody bungalow like an old lag on a chain gang. So, come on, why was you so upset that night?'

'I couldn't sleep. I... I went for a walk.'

'Funny sort of walk to leave you in a state like that – crying, and with your face covered in God knows what. So, what was it? A fight? It wouldn't hurt you to tell me, and tell me the truth for once. And turn that bloody telly off.'

Gwynedd did as she was told, and then returned to the sofa, where Sam had slept back in the good old days.

She told him the truth, but not the whole truth, giving him a highly edited account of her visit to the camp. She told him that she had been suspicious that something strange was going on and that the Mangles were involved. She had been out to their camp, to 'check it out' and thought they were keeping a lot of dogs out there.

The old man listened, and remained calm. When she had finished, he said, 'It's a load of half-truths you've given me, but we'll argue about that later. Well, I'll tell you what I think, and then we'll both forget about it, and you'll go there no more. I'm not saying this is facts, now. This is only what I think. I don't know those Mangles. Don't want to. But I can guess. And I can draw on what I do know.' He paused, as though he was reluctant to start on his tale. Then he took as deep a breath as his years of smokes allowed, as though summoning up ancient strength from deep inside. 'Forty years and more ago, there were some wild and bad things went on round here. Cruel things. Things decent folk would be ashamed to have anything to do with. But they happened. Men would go up into the woods – badger-drawing. Take a few dogs with them... terriers, mostly. They'd send a dog down the old badger's sett, find him out...then they'd dig the poor beast out of the ground and have a bit of sport with him...least, that's what they called it.'

'You think that's what the Mangles do?' said Gwynedd.

'Not likely now. There's precious few badgers left hereabouts. They was mostly gassed. I'm telling you about things that happened when I was a boy. There were farmers up in the hills – a few of them – who'd arrange cockfights. Dig a shallow pit, chuck a couple of fighting birds in it, and let them tear each other to pieces. But the worst was dog fights.' He paused, and made a face. 'I went once. Must have been younger than you. My own father took me. Up Builth way. I'll never forget it. It was all secret, of course. Word of mouth told people where to go. You didn't put up posters for a thing like that. It was in a barn. They'd fenced off the fighting arena with bales of hay, and stuck netting all around it, so's everyone got a good view of the entertainment. Mind you, it was hard to see much until your eyes got used to it. See, they lit the place with just a few hurricane lamps. And the fighting...' Again he paused, as though his memory was reluctant to recall all the details. 'They'd have dogs matched against each other...champion fighters, famous, some of them. Then they'd take bets as to which dog would win. Lot of money involved – they weren't all poor farmers that went to watch. I saw men staking a week's wages on a dog – five pound notes, even. There was plenty of drink about, too. Lot of blokes wanted drink inside them to summon up the brute courage you need for a filthy business like that.'

'What happened to the dogs?' said Gwynedd.

'They were specially bred, trained for fighting. Oh, there were one or two poor little beggars they put in the ring just to start the ball rolling. To get the blood flowing, you might say. They didn't last long. Torn to pieces. You don't want to know about that.' He stared at her, with his eyes wide open, as though suddenly aware that he wasn't merely talking to himself. 'But the major event of the evening would be between two champions – two dogs that had already had their share of kills. That was when the real betting took place, when no one could know for sure what the outcome would be. Each dog had its own way of fighting, see. Some went for the head, for the nose. Others were chest fighters. Others went for the leg. And they fought till one lost its nerve and would fight no longer. Often as not, the loser got away with its life, though chances were its owner would take the shotgun to it once the fight was over. The dog would be no good for anything after that, you see. Crippled, blinded, its nerve gone. Kinder to put it out of its misery, maybe.'

'But didn't anyone put a stop to all this?'

'Like who?'

'The police.'

Dave was scornful. 'The police? Not them. They were in it up to their helmets. There was an inspector used to come all the way from Merthyr to place his bets and watch the fun. The others...they didn't want to know. And neither do you. You don't get mixed up in any of this, Gwynedd. It's an evil thing, and they're evil and dangerous men that organise it.' He took out his tobacco and ciggie papers. 'And so it's come back, as evil does. You might have thought football would have put a stop to all that. Or telly. Better to stay home and watch any one of those poncey celebrity programmes than get involved in that.'

He lit his smoke, still gazing straight at her. 'Now –

put all this out of your mind. It happens, and there's nothing we can do about it but keep out of its way and not go looking for trouble.'

'Are you saying the Mangles hold dog fights?'

'I'm not saying anything. It's none of my business and it's none of yours.'

A question had been forming in Gwynedd's mind. She risked asking it. 'Is this why you won't have a dog?'

He covered his mouth with his hand. She could see his eyes. God almighty, was he blinking back tears? Eventually he answered her. 'That's it. See, that night, my dad didn't just take me to the fight. He took my dog...my own dog. And the poor little bugger... I've never had another dog since that bloody night. And don't you ever have one, Gwynedd. Not unless you can make sure nobody's ever going to take it from you.' He sighed again. 'Now, then,' he said, straightening his back and lifting his head, 'go and get us a cup of tea, and forget all I've told you.'

It was the longest conversation they had ever had, and there was a lot in it that she needed to think about. But that would have to wait for later. There was no time now. All that talk had eaten into what had already been scheduled as a crowded day, and was now stuffed to the brim. She was 100% certain that the Mangles were involved in dog-fights, and that Len's talk of "Friday" that night back in August referred to just such an event. She was 95% certain that Ben's life was at risk. And she was 150% certain that she wouldn't take the slightest notice of Dave's warnings and instructions.

She had to poke her nose in, and fast. She had to pay another visit to the Mangles. She *had* to find out what was going on.

Meanwhile, she had to get Dave's bloody mug of tea. She swore at the kettle, urging it to boil. She dipped the tea bag in the boiling water, stirred in milk and sugar, and hurried to the front room. He was already lost in the world of daytime TV, and she got no word of thanks.

Ten o'clock. Six hours and twenty seven minutes before she was due in Llandrindod to meet Sam. She could do it. She'd have to, even though it also involved a trip to the library before her raid on the Mangles camp. Brain work and action, research and danger... a good mixture... if there was time. She slung a scarf round her neck and jogged all the way down the lane on her way to the library, not caring if the Mangles were at home. The absence of the SUV suggested that they weren't.

The librarian tried not to show surprise, for Gwynedd Hughes had rarely visited the place since compulsory visits in junior school days.

'I need to look up something on the Net,' said Gwynedd.

'Is this for school?' said the librarian, doubtfully.

'Oh, yes,' said Gwynedd. 'It's a project. About animals.'

The librarian directed her to a computer, logged on, and fussily accessed the web for her, saying that she just wanted to make sure that all was well. Then she stayed by Gwynedd's side. Gwynedd knew what was going on. The nosey cow didn't trust her, reckoned she was up to some no-good porno-surfing. So she tapped in COW, dutifully opened up the first two websites, and waited until the librarian's attention had been taken by a regular customer. Then she entered DOG FIGHGTS. After a little coaching from the search engine, she tapped in DOG FIGHTS.

She was offered several thousand sites. Most of the first two pages had more to do with combat aircraft in the Second World War. She refined her search to CRIMNAL DOG FIGHTS. After a little more coaching, she tapped in CRIMINAL DOG FIGHTS.

The next half-hour revealed to her the sickening details of a bloody, sinister and brutal sport that seemed to have spread world-wide. She learnt of dog fights across the world – from the United States to Japan (where it was legal), from Australia to Russia - and in Britain. Dave had been right, it was a foul and bestial sport. Dog fights were held in warehouses, on allotments, even in school playgrounds after hours. The fearsome statistics rippled across the screen as she stared at it, horrified. One in three combatants was killed. The dogs were trained to attack even when their opponents were wounded, surrendering, dying. They fought on when they could barely crawl across the ring; when they had pierced their own lips with their fangs; when the entire muzzle had been torn away, leaving just cartilage from the nose and a bare lower jaw. She read of a 38-pound pit bull terrier, at a fight in Florida, whose fawn-coloured coat had been etched with so many scars that it looked as though the bitch had run headfirst through a plate-glass window...several times. The only mercy shown was the gun shot that blew the bitch's brains out.

Gwynedd read on. The fights could last for up to two hours. In parts of the States, the organisers played church music over public address systems to drown the noise of the slaughter – and to suggest a very different reason for the gathering. Winners – as well as losers – often died hours or even days after a contest, of loss of blood, or shock, dehydration, exhaustion or infection. The lucky ones were shot or strung up... that made her think of the foxes in the wood. Most fights involved gambling, and the venues were often used for drug deals – marijuana, coke, date-rape drugs. Crowds of two hundred or more paid to watch the stomach-churning torture. Was this how the Mangles had raised the money to pay for Sam's cottage?

The librarian re-appeared. 'And how are you getting on?' she said.

Gwynedd hastily shut down the system. 'Fine, thanks,' she muttered. 'I've had enough.'

She hurried out of the library, sick with shock and fear and anger, knowing that – even if she had wanted to, which she decidedly didn't - she couldn't now obey Dave's orders. She'd have to go looking for trouble – not just for Sam's sake. After what Dave had told her, and what she'd just learnt in the library, Gwynedd realised she was doing this for Ben's sake as well. That bloomin' dog was what this was all about.

Her appetite for drama was sharpened by the knowledge that she and Sam were ultimately on their own in this. There was no one they could turn to for help. She had promised Dave she'd have nothing to do with the Mangles. Well, that promise had gone out of the window unless she was smart enough and quick enough to get what she wanted without being caught. And, from what Dave had said about that Inspector from Merthyr back in the old days, the police weren't to be trusted. Who else was there? Rhayader was a small community. No one wanted to stir up trouble by starting a row with a neighbour, or by betraying a friend or customer to the authorities. Sure, there were plenty of nosey-parkers in the town, but they just wanted to know what was going on. They didn't want to do anything about it.

For all her excitement, Gwynedd was experienced enough to know that things had to go on as normal back in the bungalow. Dave had to have his din-dins. There were a couple of good Welsh lamb chops in the freezer compartment of the fridge. She dug them out and plunged them into a bowl of warm water to defrost. In the garden, there were still plenty of potatoes to be dug, and pickings to be had from a row or two of mud spattered spinach. She went out, lifted a few potatoes, cut some spinach, then returned to the kitchen to wash them.

She'd give him an early dinner. It was nearly eleven. She'd get it started now, so's it would be out of the way well before twelve. That would still give her nearly two and a half hours to take a second quick look at the Mangles' old camp and get to Llandrindod to meet Sam's train. What she needed most was information. She had to know if Ben was still alive, and, if so, where the Mangles were keeping him. You can't steal anything unless you know where to steal it from. The moment Dave had started on about dog fights, she had known that she had to persuade Sam that Ben had to be snatched from the Mangles and whisked away, to some place of safety that she hadn't thought of yet. And that meant she had to pay another visit to the camp. With luck, Ben wouldn't be there. He'd be at the cottage, where it would be easier to grab hold of him. If Ben was at the camp, well, that would make life both hard and dangerous and she'd have to think of some way of stealing Ben while avoiding the other canine company.

She scrubbed the potatoes and popped them in a pan of cold water. As soon as Dave finished his dinner, she'd be off. It was risky, she knew that, but Gwynedd's spirits always rose, blindly optimistic, to any challenge. She'd faced the Mangles at the cottage and got away. She'd been to the camp once already, and got away with no more harm done than the fright of her life. There would have to be a close encounter of the third kind, and, if it was a case of "three strikes, you're out", well that was the way luck ran. She'd been unlucky so far in not finding out exactly what was going on and exactly where Ben was being kept. This time, if things went well, she'd both find Ben and discover the murky secret of the Mangles. And if things went really badly? Then there'd be no one to meet Sam off the train, and a gruesome front-page article for the next edition of the local paper. What a way to go!

A visit to the camp would take time. This could be no hurried expedition. As Mr Richards used to say when they played Frozen Footsteps during wet playtimes in the Hall at Junior School: 'Speed is the enemy of stealth'. The closer she intruded to the heart of the Mangles's camp, the slower her progress must be. And, once there, she had no idea how long her search might take. Say – fifteen minutes to get to the forest, twenty minutes to get through the forest, half an hour for a snoop round, then another twenty-five minutes to get back. In all that was…well, this was more like being at blooming school. Doing sums at half term – if dear old Mr Richards could see her now! 'That's not like you, Gwynedd Hughes,' she muttered to herself. 'And don't just rely on your pretty little head, neither. Get yourself a piece of paper and a pencil.' She wrote the figures down on an old envelope and added them together. It seemed to come to ninety minutes. Say, an hour and three quarters, to be on the safe side.

God, was that all? Easy. She could clear up Dave's dinner, do the camp and still catch the Llandrindod bus up at the car park in town just before two. And, if she was back early from the camp, she could smarten herself up and give darling Sam's lovely blue eyes something to feast on.

She prodded the lamb chops. The outsides were nice and flabby but inside they was hard as coal. Give 'em a bit of a thaw in the oven, speed things up. Then, once they'd thawed, she'd fry them up in a pan with plenty of dripping, the way Dave used to like.

Meanwhile, put the spuds on to boil...

The meal was not a success. Dave had barely returned from his regular morning stroll into Rhayader to buy the *Daily Mirror* when she called him to the table. He sat down and proceeded to complain about everything. The spinach was too dry, far too gritty, hadn't been washed properly. The potatoes were too wet and their skins were dirty. The chops were burnt on the outside and raw in the middle. He was mollified a little by a plate of tinned pears, but was still moaning when he shuffled to his favourite chair to read the racing pages, mark his card, and smoke himself to sleep.

'Set yourself on fire one of these days,' she said. 'And the bungalow and me as well.'

'What's got into you?' he said. 'It's not gone twelve. Worse than hospital catering, this is.'

'I'm popping out,' said Gwynedd. 'See some mates. Er...by the way, Sam's coming this evening.'

'Sam?'

'Sam Harper. Him and his mum went to Bristol. He stayed here before. You like him.' She left the lie hanging in the air and hurried from the room.

CHAPTER 12

This time, she approached the Mangles' camp from further up the valley, where there was thicker cover all the way to the edge of the clearing. She moved fast, making some noise but not enough to matter. She was prepared for trouble, with her mobile in her pocket, charged and in credit. Moving through the wood in the muted daylight, she could see that several of the trees had gashes on them, with teeth marks right through the bark and into the trunk, just as they'd been in the clearing with the dead foxes. The broken branches lying on the ground had been savaged. Well, thanks to the Net, this time she knew what all that was about. Someone had been out to toughen up at least one dog's jaws before a fight.

Gwynedd hurried on, until she was really close. There were sounds of activity in the camp, comings and goings. The Mangles were not alone in the woods. She heard a car... no, two cars, coming up the rough track that led from the valley road. She nipped behind a dead tree, steadying her breathing, and trying to shut her ears to all other sounds. The cars stopped. The engines were switched off. Doors opened and slammed shut. Squinting round the tree, she saw Len hurry from the caravan to the cars. A moment later he returned with three men – two large, one small. They climbed into one of the removal trucks. She *had* to get closer, close enough to hear what they were saying…

They were soon back, stomping down the tailboard of the truck. The large men shook hands with Len, got into one of the cars, and reversed slowly down the track, back the way they'd come. Mags came out of the caravan to join Len and the small man. Len went to put his arms round her, as though something good had happened, but she pushed him away. Then the three of them fetched four large wooden crates from the truck, and placed them in the centre of the clearing.

Gwynedd moved in. To her right, there was a pine with branches drooping to the ground, creating a kind of wigwam of spindly wood and needles. It would be painful work, but if she could wriggle inside that, she would be much nearer, and still be well hidden. She moved forward on fists and toes, like a monkey. Slowly… slowly, now… not too fast. She reached the wigwam and lowered her stomach to the ground. Shit! That was a pine needle digging into her hand. Wriggle… wriggle… wriggle… there! The best view yet of the camp.

She still couldn't make out what the crates contained, but she could see that each crate was continually wobbling. There was live things inside them crates –

and it didn't take a genius to guess that the live things was dogs.

The small man was issuing instructions to Len and Mags, instructions that they obeyed without argument. Gwynedd didn't recognise the man as anyone from the town or any of the houses round about, so he was an outsider. He was smartly dressed, though the mud in the clearing wasn't doing his posh pants or his shiny shoes much good. He was fair-haired, pink-faced...not a countryman, very much a townie, neat in his clothes and the way he moved. He clearly knew what he was doing.

She could see him nodding as he inspected the crates, as though pleased with what he saw. He returned several times to the crate that had been brought out first. Gwynedd heard the word 'champion', and a phrase she couldn't quite catch... something to do with 'bring the punters in...' From one of the other trucks, Len and Mags fetched a platform with what looked like a giant set of bathroom scales on it. They set up the platform next to the crates, and lifted the first crate on to it. Something was being weighed. Gwynedd risked moving a little nearer.

The small man took a pen and notebook from his jacket pocket and jotted something down. He and Len lifted the crate off the scales and placed it beside the platform. Len pulled on a pair of heavy-duty gloves, and shot back a pair of bolts, to open the crate. For a second or two, nothing happened. Len bent down, gently clapped his gloved hands together, and whistled softly.

'Come on, Prince. Out you come, my lovely mutt. Got to make sure you're in prime condition for tomorrow.'

The dog that strutted from the crate was heavily built, squat, tough, muscular – a dog with a lot of pit bull terrier in it, ferocity personified. In her wigwam, Gwynedd flattened her body against the ground.

Len clipped a heavy chain on to the dog's collar. He led it to the side, away from the small man and the scales. The dog snarled, but was half choked by Len pulling on the chain.

'Attaboy, Prince,' he said, admiringly.

The small, neat man now weighed the empty crate and made another note in his book. He appeared to be making a calculation. More sums - Gwynedd guessed he was subtracting the weight of the empty cage from the weight of the cage and dog, to give him the weight of the dog. Back in the old days, that would have given her poor teacher something to think about – Gwynedd Hughes making use of applied mathematics.

The crate was placed back on the ground. Len dragged the dog over to it, and then fished something out of his pocket and threw it in the crate. 'Get it, Prince,' he said, and unclipped the dog's chain. The dog clambered into the crate. Gwynedd was close enough to hear a chomping, slobbering, masticating sound. Len then bolted the crate shut. 'Bit of old horse meat, Prince. You'll get something fresher tomorrow.'

The small man slipped his pen and notebook back into his pocket, and helped Len carry the crate and the dog back into the truck. Mags had disappeared with the scales. The two men squatted down to inspect the contents of the other crates. At each crate, Len murmured a few remarks to the small man, who nodded, but said nothing. Gwynedd caught the words 'get things going...', 'overture and beginners' (whatever that meant), the word 'champion' again, and 'starters'. They made little sense to her. But several times she heard the words 'tomorrow night'.

The meeting came to an end. The small man shook hands with Len, got back into his car and drove slowly away. Len loaded the remaining crates back into the lorry – clearly, if there were dogs inside them, none of the poor creatures weighed anything like as much as Prince. Having done that, Len glanced around, took off his gloves, dusted his hands and went back to the caravan.

Gwynedd allowed herself a sigh of relief and eased her body slowly out from under the wigwam. As well as bad meat, she could smell urine, a stink like the derelict kiosk on the recreation ground, where the lads of the town pee-ed after they'd drunk too much on Saturday nights. There was a clinking noise as her foot struck an empty tin, one of many scattered about the ground.

And then there was another noise. Her mobile phone rang. God above, that was scary, but they couldn't have heard that in the caravan. No way. She dropped to the ground, snatching the mobile from her pocket. The blessed thing was still blaring away. She switched it off, and started to snake backwards, away from the camp. She was doing fine. Just a few more metres and it would be safe enough to get up and run.

An enormous dog burst out at her from behind the trees. For a split second terror paralysed her. She couldn't move. Then she staggered helplessly backwards as the dog again leapt at her, coming so close that she could almost taste its breath. But each time it leapt something was jerking it back, restraining it, twisting its head away from her face. The dog dug its back legs into the ground and sprang once more, only to be pulled back a third time. As Gwynedd recoiled from it, she glimpsed a chain running from the dog's neck to a sack on the ground, and prayed that the far end of the chain was fastened to some great weight inside the sack.

The beast leapt and snarled. Gwynedd turned to flee. Her feet slipped on the carpet of pine needles, and she stumbled over a tree root. She heard a voice cut through the dog's growling roar. But the voice was coming from the wrong direction, not from behind her but from somewhere ahead, from the way she desperately wanted to go.

'What is it, Beauty? Fox?... Rat?... Well, I'm blowed... it's a two-legged rat! What shall we do, Beauty? How about we grab her, and then I slip your chain?...'

Len grabbed Gwynedd and pinned her arms behind her back while Mags went through her pockets. All they found was her mobile, which Len hurled into the undergrowth.

'You can look for it later,' he said.

They slung her in the back of one of the removal trucks and left her there, locked in the dark, the damp and the cold. If this was meant to be a softening up exercise, it worked. Gwynedd had no idea how long they kept her there, but it was enough for her imagination to run riot. At first she feared they were going to kill her... strangle her, knife her, throw her to the dogs. She tried to convince herself this was rubbish. The Mangles weren't idiots. Their own lives weren't at stake. All they were doing was getting some dog fight together. Why kill someone over that? But if this was about a dog fight, there was money involved, and plenty of people killed for money.

She dragged herself to a corner of the truck and sat on the floor, her knees drawn up protectively in front, her back pressed against the metal sides. She heard scuffling noises, indicating the presence of other creatures. Dogs? No, rats, more likely. How many of them? And how hungry? She told herself to hold on. Rats wouldn't kill her. Nor the Mangles. They'd have to let you go sometime. She kept reminding herself how many times in the past adults had threatened her and how many times she'd called their bluff. This time, it didn't work. She failed to convince herself that her fears were rubbish. She was shaking with fear. If the Mangles wanted to kill her, they would.

Reaching deep inside her for a last nugget of courage, she raised herself on to her hands and knees. The scuttling feet around her broke into a neurotic stampede, but she hung grimly on, and managed a strange kind of laugh when she felt nothing bigger than a mouse run over her foot. She had no ma to cry for, no dad to come galloping to her rescue. No one. It was down to her. Keep going. For Chrissake, she told herself. Keep going!

A long time passed.

She didn't hear them coming, but a key rattled in a lock and one of the doors opened. Against the muted daylight, Gwynedd saw two figures... the Mangles. The door was closed and the truck was plunged into darkness. Suddenly, a bright light blazed into her eyes. She did her best to shield them with her hands. For a while, nothing was said then, out of the darkness behind the light came Len's voice.

'If Beauty's chain had been a few links longer, that impertinent little nose and big mouth of yours would have been dog food. Dear, oh dear. You keep getting in the way,' he said. 'What do we have to do to make you listen?'

A fist was pushed under her chin, forcing her head up so that she had to look into the light. She trembled, more frightened than she had ever been in her life.

There was a chilling silence in the truck. The fist was removed from her chin and a large, tough hand smacked her on the cheek. Gwynedd whimpered.

Len laughed. 'You know, Magsie, if there's one thing I hope the vicar will say... the vicar who presides one day at my funeral service...'

'Don't, Len,' said Mags. 'You know what the idea of

your ever departing this life does to me. Gives me real hope, and I get this excitement welling up inside.'

'...I hope the dear vicar will say, "Here lies Len Franklin, the most forgiving creature God ever fashioned from the clay of life".'

'He will,' said Mags. 'The vicar *will* say that. I'll make him.'

'So – we are *not* gonna bring unhappiness to this young life.'

'What a lovely sentiment,' said Mags. Just for a second, Gwynedd thought she heard what sounded like relief in the woman's voice.

'We're going to teach her a lesson. We're going to show her what might-have-been.'

He grabbed Gwynedd, hauled her to her feet, dragged her to the tailboard of the truck, opened the door, and shoved her out. She fell in the mud, and he yanked her upright before she had time to even think of making a bolt for it.

The Mangles marched Gwynedd across to the biggest of the trucks, and dragged her inside, closing the doors behind them. It was dark, Gwynedd could hardly see a thing. She didn't need to. The deafening roar of snarling and growling all around told her what to expect. Len forced her to the very back of the truck, and switched on the powerful torch.

'Let me introduce you to the sweetest natured little doggies in the world.'

'Get a move on, Len.' Mags sounded impatient, as though she wanted to put an end to this business.

'Forgive me, babe.' He grabbed Gwynedd by the hair and forced her head down till it was level with the wire mesh of one of the crates. 'Gwynedd, dear... meet Lad.'

Snarling hysterically, the dog inside the crate flung itself at the thick wire mesh, shoving its muzzle forward until it seemed its face must be forced through the mesh like meat through a mincer. Len brought his fist crunching down on the top of the crate. The dog withdrew its head. 'That's what we do with those that shove their faces where they ain't wanted, eh, Lad?' He turned to Gwynedd and shook her again. 'Understand?' There was a pause while he calmed himself. 'Now, let's meet some of the others.'

Much the same process was repeated at another crate. Gwynedd's spirits rose a fraction. Threats and more threats, a vicious shaking, and a slap in the face. That was all so far. Her eyes were becoming accustomed to the darkness inside the truck. In one corner she could see some kind of treadmill, far too big for a hamster, far too small for a human being, just the right size for a dog. Her fears retreated further. This wasn't a death sentence. It was more of what she'd already suffered. And it was taking up a lot of time. They'd have to let her go eventually.

She took in all the details. She knew from the Net what this treadmill was for – to build up a fighting dog's stamina and endurance. Some dogs covered the equivalent of ten miles a day in machines like that. And that electric fan suspended above the treadmill, with the cable from it running away through a hole in the roof of the truck – that was to cool the dog down as it pounded away. Hanging on the walls were all manner of leashes and chains, collars and muzzles. Maybe that was safety equipment.

'Each one has a special place in our hearts...'

More snarling, more shouting, more teeth and slobber. The Mangles were no different from teachers – always overdoing the threats.

But they moved to a third crate. It was the moment when Gwynedd's blood ran cold. For a second or two she was convinced that, this time, the dog she was about to see would be Ben – perhaps a Ben hideously altered by a few weeks as a prisoner of the Mangles. But the massive beast that cavorted with fury only a tongue's length away from her face was the dog that had so nearly got her, the dog at the end of the chain. She felt herself once again staring death in the face.

'That's Beauty,' said Len. 'Wonderful dog. Eats anything I give him...rabbits, crows, sticks, Mags' old clothes, other dogs – when times are hard. And does everything I tell him...sits, begs, rolls over, kills, everything. Like to see him in action?'

Gwynedd flinched.

'No, no, dear. I'm just joking.'

'Get on with it, Len.' Mags lit a cigarette and took a quick puff. 'This is no bloody time for jokes.'

'No. Beauty won't do you any harm. Unless I tell him to. And then he will.' His voice hardened. 'Make no mistake about that. He'll kill you if I tell him, and by God, on my own blood I say this, I will tell him if you ever come near this place again, or if you ever say one word to anyone about what you've seen here.' His face relaxed into a grotesque smile. 'I know what you're thinking – if Beauty did kill you, what would happen to us, eh? Well, don't you worry about that. You see, we'd make sure there were no witnesses. Not only that, if Beauty was really hungry, there wouldn't even be any evidence, let alone witnesses. You're dead. Suppose the police come to me, tell me that apparently my little Beauty here's savaged some poor young girl to death. I get fined. Poor old Beauty gets put down. Breaks my heart, maybe. But I got other dogs. I'll get over it. Meanwhile, you're still dead and you ain't got other lives and you won't get over it.'

They took her out of the truck. 'So you see, dear...' Mags spoke quietly as she peered into Gwynedd's frightened face, '...you'd best do as Len says.' For one mad moment, Gwynedd thought that Mags was going to say "please".

Len's eyes narrowed. 'Half a tick, Mags,' he said. 'I'm forgetting that Gwynedd here is an old friend of that Sam you're so fond of, and our little Benny.' He smiled. 'Well, that makes our job a whole lot easier. You blab to anyone about our little Home for Waifs and Strays, and dear old Bennikins becomes din-dins for Beauty and the others. How about that? Keep your trap shut and Ben lives. Open your trap and it's "Bye-bye Bennikins". Don't take no notice of those threats I made about setting Beauty on you. Did I really say I would? Dreadful! How could I! A threat like that could give you bleedin' nightmares. No! You just think of Ben. And do remember, dear, that we know where you live.'

'Len often takes Beauty for walks at night. When it's all quiet and there's no one about. It has to be then, because Beauty gets nervous with strangers. They bring out the beast in him. As they do my Len. But, you see, my Len could easy walk Beauty up your way. And he will if there's any trouble.' Mags took another puff on her cigarette. Was her hand shaking... just a little?

'Yes,' said Len. 'Yes, I will.'

Gwynedd experienced a flicker of hope that the terrifying ordeal was about to come to an end. They'd made their threats. Now it was time to let her go. She had only to hold herself together a bit longer and she would be legging it out of the hell-hole and breathing freedom.

'She thinks we're done, Mags. I can see it in her face. What she needs is another spell in the rat-house. Just to think things over. For a night or so.'

They took her back to the truck where she had first been imprisoned, and locked her once more in the dark. She hadn't the spirit to kick or thump the sides of the lorry, to shout or scream, to make any kind of protest. She dragged herself to the same corner in which she had cowered last time, as though there might be comfort in the familiar, and sat there, shivering with cold and terror and exhaustion. She knew they would have to let her go in the end, but she was losing faith in her own ability to survive until that end was reached. If she did scream now, it would be for mercy.

Without her mobile, she had no way of judging the passage of time. She tried counting seconds but lost heart long before she got to a hundred. What was the point? Her shivering turned to shaking, and she began to weep silently.

Later – she had no idea how much later – she again heard the sound of a key being fitted into the padlock that held the truck doors closed. They were coming back. She could take no more misery. She would beg them to let her go. The door opened, enough to admit a crack of light.

'Gwynedd!' The voice was urgent. It was also young, and one she knew well.

She clambered to her feet, and stumbled towards the light and the doors.

'Shut up! Quiet as you can! If they hear us, I've had it.'

It was Mollie. She opened the door a little wider and held out her hand. Gwynedd grasped it and squeezed out of the truck. She stood, blinking in what little light there was, while Mollie fastened the truck doors and then hurled the key into the undergrowth. 'That'll take some finding,' she whispered. 'Come on, and keep your mouth shut till I tell you.'

They hurried from the camp into the trees, Mollie leading the way. Gwynedd had difficulty keeping pace with her, for she was cold to the bone and her own body was limp with tiredness. Not until they reached the very edge of the wood did Mollie stop.

'Now then,' she said. 'Let's talk for once. You don't like me an' I don't like you. You're all mouth until it comes to the real showdown and then we don't hear nothing out of you. But you stood by the deal we made, that night when you come looking for trouble here, and I ain't forgotten that.'

'I never made a deal,' said Gwynedd.

'Don't be so bloody stupid. Of course you did. You didn't say nothing about my mum and dad after that night, and that's why I'm saving you now. But it's the last time. You're one big bloody fool, coming back here, and you can thank Vinnie for your escape. He's been loping around, looking for you for the last three hours – said you weren't at home, nor at the Leisure Centre, didn't know where you could be. I couldn't believe you'd be dumb enough to come here again, but you're always full of surprises. I got back just in time to see mum and dad locking you up, waited till they were brewing tea in the caravan, and then chanced it. And that's it. I'm not taking any more risks on your behalf, whatever you do.'

'What about you?'

'What d'you care!' Mollie stared fiercely at her. 'You don't care what happens to anyone so long as you can act like you owned this place and Sam Harper with it. Got some mad plan to rescue his pathetic dog, have you? Forget it. There ain't gonna be no Ben after tomorrow night. And don't even think of going to the police...'

'I won't. I swear I won't!'

'No,' said Mollie. 'I don't believe even you are that stupid. You just keep quiet about everything. Deal?'

Gwynedd nodded. 'But what about you?'

'They won't kill me, if that's what you mean. Except for the dogs, I'm all they've got. Besides, Len reckons I'll be bringing in money in a couple of years. Right – if anyone asks, you ain't seen me. I've been in town all afternoon. You'll have to think what you've been doing. And for all our sakes, come up with something better than your usual crap stories. Now, piss off.'

Gwynedd hurried home as fast as her aching body would allow. The moment she reached the bungalow, she checked the time by Dave's alarm clock. It was ten past five. Sam's train had arrived at Llandrindod nearly two hours ago.

CHAPTER 13

She found him down by the river, near the empty campsite. He was sitting on their old rock, eating something out of a brown paper bag. Though she was still shivering with shock and fear, she noticed how carefully he was keeping the crumbs off his designer jacket. Even with eyes still wet with tears, she noted the pricey new trainers. He waved to her as she hurried up to him.

'Have a Welsh cake,' he said. 'The woman in the baker's gave me two... one for me and one for what she called my "sweetheart".' He imitated a Welsh woman's voice. 'I think they're a bit old, and she was trying to get rid of them. But how about this!' He waved what was clearly a most superior mobile phone in her face. 'Plays music, videos... takes photos. You want to send emails? Surf the Net?...' He looked up, expecting to see envy and admiration in her face. Only then did he realise that something was wrong. 'Are you all right?'

She might have held on, but finding him there of all places, waiting for her, was too much. 'No, I'm not,' she said, and burst into tears.

He put his arms round her. She grabbed him and held on for longer than was comfortable.

'You're late,' he mumbled into her sweater.

She continued to cry.

'I mean, not that it matters. But you are late, and we were supposed to meet at the station in Llandrindod. I called you from the train, on your mobile. Just to check you'd be there – but there was no answer.'

She broke from him and lashed out with her fist. He'd made the call that had given her away, and led to the loss of her mobile.

'It was you,' she said. 'You did it!' Then she fell back into his arms, and what she hoped were the last sobs left in her, poured forth. He manoeuvred their bodies so that they could both sit safely on the rock.

'What is it? What's wrong?'

She gave him a highly edited account of her afternoon. She told him that she'd gone to the camp, that the Mangles had grabbed her and given her a hard time. She said nothing about the violence, nothing about Mollie, and nothing about the loss of her mobile. If she told him about that, he'd want to be the perfect gent and go looking for it, which would be bloody dangerous. Most of all, she did what she could to play down her fears for Ben. She told him about the dog fights, that there was to be one tomorrow night but she didn't know where. He immediately wanted to know about Ben. She stumbled a little over the lie that there was no way Ben would be involved.

Even so, it was difficult for Sam to take it all in. He guessed she'd had a bad time, for her voice trembled as she spoke, and there were moments when she began to cry again. She looked at the sleeve of his posh new designer jacket, and noted the splashes of tears. 'I'm ruining your lovely jacket,' she said.

'Doesn't matter.'

She lost her self-control, and started shaking and crying again. 'There were these dogs... terrible dogs. Killers! I thought I was gonna be killed!'

She slid down the rock and sat on the grass, her head on her knees, her hands on her head, her shoulders up round her ears.

'Tell me more about Ben,' he said.

'Don't know where he is.'

'We've got to find him and rescue him,' he said.

'No, Sam. Please!'

'Yep. If he's not at the camp, then he must be at the cottage. All we have to do is wait till they let him out, or leave the back door open, and call him. He'll come if I call him.'

'Suppose they don't let him out? Suppose they don't leave the back door open? Not everyone's as careless as you. Suppose he's chained up? I can't see the Mangles letting any creature run free. Even their guard dogs are kept on chains... thank God.' She recalled Beauty's muzzle snapping shut within a whisker of her face.

'You say all this dog fight business is set for tomorrow night and that Ben's not involved. Then, once the Mangles have left for the fight, we'll break into the

151

cottage and get Ben. It's not stealing,' he said. 'He's my dog.'

'You've not seen the Mangles like I have. They'd kill anyone that tried to get in their way.'

'You keep talking about killing. Nobody's going to kill us... All right, all right,' he said, quickly. 'Have it your way. Maybe the Mangles do kill people. Maybe the woods are full of corpses. We can still save Ben.'

She shook her head and said nothing. There was an awkward silence, broken by the church clock striking six.

'Oh, God,' she said, miserably. 'It's Dave's tea time... and he had an early dinner.' She took a deep breath and drew the sleeve of her grubby, patched sweater across her eyes and under her nose. She looked up at him. 'Have you got any money?'

Like most totally unexpected questions, it got an honest answer. 'Lots. My mum gave me more than enough. I think she expected I'd get everything wrong on the trains, and end up having to get a taxi here from London or something. I mean... that's pathetic. She's OK, but she always expects the worst will happen.'

Lucky Sam, she thought. To have someone looking after him, someone who tried to keep one step ahead of trouble.

'I bet your Becky was dead keen to get rid of you,' she said. 'I bet she's already at it with her Martin. I bet that money was a bribe.' Gwynedd was recovering.

'Bollocks,' he said. 'It was in case of emergencies.'

Bollocks? She'd never heard him use that word

before. Bristol was changing him. She wanted to know more about that, but there was no time right now.

'This is an emergency,' she said. 'A bloody Red Alert emergency. You don't know what Dave's like when he don't get his tea.' She grabbed Sam's arm. 'Come on, let's go down the chippie.'

'OK. But just let me show you how this works.' He was fiddling with his mobile again. 'Let me take some photos of you...'

'Not looking like this, please, Sam.'

He put the mobile away.

They joined the queue in the warm fug of the North Street chippie, breathing in the heady scent of hot cooking oil. In the queue, Gwynedd examined Sam's face.

'What are you staring at?'

'Your ugly gob,' she said. 'It's got worse since you've been away.'

It wasn't true, but it had changed. The soft lines that she remembered so well from Junior school days were firmer, maybe a tiny bit rougher. His eyes were darker. There was what looked like soft stubble on his chin.

'You been shaving?'

'Certainly. Once this morning, once on the train, and due for another one any minute now.'

She laughed, and was pleased to see that her laugh had attracted the Paki lad's attention. The queue shuffled forward.

'What are the girls like in Bristol?'

'Well, they're not like you or Mollie, that's for sure.'

'What's Mollie got to do with it?'

'To do with what?'

'Have you come here to see me or Mollie?' She couldn't help herself.

'I've come here to see Ben,' he said. 'And you,' he added, too late.

There was another awkward silence before he said: 'Are you still fighting with Mollie?'

He had no idea what was going on, and she couldn't tell him, but at least she could answer his question truthfully, which made a change. 'No,' she said.

'Good.'

She was angry again. Why was that good? 'Why do you keep going on about Mollie?' she said.

He sighed. 'I simply said the girls in Bristol aren't like you or Mollie.'

She didn't like his sigh because she didn't understand it, and she didn't know what to say.

They reached the counter, and she was face to face with the Paki lad.

'And what can Saqui get you tonight?'

'Saqui?'

'It's my name,' said the Paki lad. 'You never ask it, but I decided to tell you. You ought to know the names of your creditors.' He saw her bewilderment. 'Creditors - those people to whom you owe money. Six pounds thirty, to be precise.'

Cheek. And all that poncey "to whom". Nobody spoke like that.

She ordered cod and chips twice, a third cod and chips laced with salt and vinegar and two pickled onions for Dave, and a couple of giant bottles of Coke, 'for me and my man.' She persuaded Sam to pay off her debt with the emergency money that Becky had given him. Her recovery was accelerating.

Hugging their warm parcels of fish and chips and taking alternate swigs from one of the Coke bottles, they hurried down South Street and headed for the bungalow. Just for one moment, drinking Coke reminded them both of the night that she and Sam had looked at Becky's photograph album in the old cottage, but they said nothing about it to each other.

She served Dave his fish and chips in the living room. Having lost all memory of the information that Gwynedd had hurled at him earlier in the day, the old man had greeted his guest with a bad-tempered 'What's he doing here?' As Gwynedd had forecast, he was in a bad mood. She poured Dave a beer, and switched on the telly. She saved the pickled onions as a parting gift, slapping them on Dave's plate just before she and Sam retreated to the kitchen to eat their tea together.

The hot, fat food did its healing work, and their old friendship found its feet. They sat in the kitchen, and talked until late.

'How are things with Mollie?' asked Sam.

'Why are you always going on about that cow Mollie?'

'Well, she's the Leader of the Pack, isn't she? You

can't exactly ignore Mollie. Least – *you* never did.'

Two different worlds, she thought. I don't know what happens in Bristol. You don't know what happens here. She'd been wrong to think that it would be easy for Sam to somehow keep in touch with his old world, but right to expect she could have no idea of what his life would be like in Bristol – there'd been a lot of talk of pizzerias, the rugger team, the problems of catching up in Spanish. As if it mattered... She suddenly realised she wasn't listening to what he was saying, and tried to tune into his words.

'... don't worry. We'll find a new home for Ben. A shed or something. And we'll fit a padlock on it to keep him secure... What?'

'Nothing,' she said.

'You pulled a face.'

'I'm fine.'

'Right. And we'll lay in a store of food.' He took money from his pocket and counted it on to the kitchen table. The fish and chips, and the settlement of Gwynedd's debt had taken a large slice out of what Becky had given him, but there still seemed to be plenty. 'We'll manage,' he said.

Saying goodnight was awkward. It had been so easy, back in the summer... Right now, spending a night together under the same roof would be strange enough, even if all had been well between them. There had been plenty of times over the last few days when she had thought about how they would say goodnight. She was going to take hold of his hands, and look at him with her head slightly down, from under her eyelids, like. Give him a little smile, but more tender than laughing. And then all he'd have to do was smile back, the same way, only not from under his eyelids 'cos that'd be silly. And then she'd lean a little towards him, and they would kiss. Not one of Vinnie's bloody kisses with his tongue lashing about down your throat like a fish on the end of a line, but gentle. And she and Sam would say goodnight like they didn't want to, and she could go to her bedroom with a feeling that something magic and lovely had happened. It wasn't much to ask.

But Sam just said it had been a long day and he was exhausted, she just said 'Me too', and left him.

She heard Sam go to the bathroom to brush his teeth. Becky would have told him to do that, probably told him every night. Not like bloody Dave. All you got from him was a belch and the slamming of his door. She stroked the bruises on her arm where the Mangles had gripped her. Inside her head she heard the violent barking and snarling of the dogs in their crates. When she closed her eyes she could still see Len's face, mouthing threats. Her hope had been that once Sam arrived she would no longer be alone in all this. Well, he was in the next room, almost within reach, and there had been all this talk from him about how they would fight back tomorrow. Had he really meant it? Maybe he had. He'd do anything for that dog. And maybe he was right. Once they'd found Ben and got him safely away, maybe there was nothing the Mangles could do. Whatever they'd threatened, all she had to do was keep out of their clutches. You couldn't be harmed by someone who couldn't reach you. There was a lesson in that.

Well, that was something. For a while she believed it, but then doubts began to crowd her thoughts. The Mangles were a tough couple. And there were all those dogs. So many dogs... never mind Sam and his long journey, she'd had a worse day than him, and far more exhausting. She wondered if he'd been truly disappointed that she hadn't been at Llandrindod station to meet him. She wished she'd paid more attention to his nattering in the chippie... Saqui, that was quite a nice name, really...

She sat up in bed. Why hadn't the Mangles taken her to the crate with the pit-bull terrier? The dog that had been weighed...what was its name? Prince, that was it. Why hadn't they threatened her with Prince? To judge from the way Len had fawned over it, talked to it, anyone would think it was the pride of his collection. And it was certainly terrifying. What was so special about it? Why had it been weighed? And what was the meaning of all that talk about 'beginners' and 'champions'? Was tomorrow night's fight going to be a big event? And, most important of all, where was it going to take place?

Long before she could come up with an answer to any of the questions, Gwynedd had fallen asleep.

CHAPTER 14

Gwynedd slept badly, with dreams that she was being pursued by a pack of marauding hounds whipped on by a mad Mollie. She woke late with a sour taste in her mouth, and the racket in her ears of Dave shouting for his mug of tea. She got up, dressed, went to the bathroom to slop water on her face, and then on to the kitchen. While the kettle boiled, she wondered what sort of a night Mollie had spent.

She took the mug of tea to Dave's room and returned to the kitchen. Sam was waiting for her. She hurried him through breakfast and out of the bungalow.

'The cottage,' he said. 'We go straight to the cottage and check that Ben's OK.'

Gwynedd had her doubts. There was plenty of danger in going to the cottage. She didn't want to face the Mangles again so soon after the trauma of yesterday, and she didn't want Sam to get in a state if Ben wasn't at the cottage. On the other hand, she desperately wanted to check up on Mollie. Cow she may be, but Mollie had taken an enormous risk in helping her get away yesterday, and it would be a relief to know that Mollie was safe.

'Well, just a quick look,' said Gwynedd. She wanted to check that Mollie was OK, but something else was pressing on her mind.

They walked hand in hand in the autumn sunshine, and had reached the bend before the cottage when they heard a powerful car engine start up. Gwynedd recognised the sound. She'd heard it all too recently.

'Quick,' she said. 'Over that gate... into the field. Now!'

They threw themselves over the gate and on to the ground, rolling over the wet grass to take cover behind the hedge. They were just in time. The black SUV drove past and accelerated up the lane, heading for the mountains.

'Mangles,' said Gwynedd.

'Let's get a picture.' He leaned over the gate and held up his mobile.

'Don't be daft.'

'It's not daft. It's evidence. Where do you reckon they're going?'

'I dunno. Cwmystwyth, maybe. Devil's Bridge.' She hoped it was all the way to Aberystwyth, then along the pier and into the sea.

'But this *is* something to do with those dog fights?'

'I dunno.' She was back to lying, and she didn't like lying to Sam.

'Come on,' he said. 'Let's have a quick look at the cottage.'

'Don't be mad.' Gwynedd brain was racing. She had suddenly realised what was pressing on her mind... something that Mollie had said in the woods yesterday. Something about 'there ain't gonna be no Ben after tomorrow night...' The Mangles were going to use him in a dog fight. Ben was going to be one of the little beggars that Dave had talked about. Ben was going to be torn to pieces.

'How's it mad?

It took Gwynedd a moment or two before she could answer him. 'Two minutes ago you were throwing yourself into the cowpats to avoid being seen by the Mangles, now you want to go blundering into their cottage.'

'You started that,' he said. 'And I thought you wanted us to find Ben.'

They hung around the cottage for twenty minutes. There was no sign of either Mollie or Ben, so they left, and wandered up into town. Sam took photos of Gwynedd every 30 seconds until she told him to stop. The rest of the way, he talked about iPods, Blackberries, sport, school, Bristol, and money. She talked about Dave, Vinnie, school, and lack of money. It seemed to Gwynedd that the distance between them was growing larger by the minute. She could scarcely bear it.

For old times sake, they went to *La Strada* for a Coke. It was a mistake.

'The last time we were here,' said Sam, 'was when you had that row with Mollie.'

'It was a row with you,' she said.

'Was it?'

'About Ben.'

'Then Mollie joined in.'

'Don't keep going on about Mollie,' she snapped.

He took another hundred photos, sent three texts, and checked his emails. She wanted to throw her Coke over him, like she'd done last time. Bloody clocks, she thought. You can't ever turn them back.

They returned to the bungalow and he took photos of her cooking Dave's dinner. When they'd eaten, they sat together at the kitchen table, while Dave watched television in the parlour.

'You know what we can do tonight?' said Sam.

She shook her head.

'Dress up and frighten people, and then come back and drink rum. Has Dave got any rum?'

She didn't catch on.

'It's Halloween,' he said. 'Don't you remember?'

She did. Those old Halloween nights, when they had descended like a gang of bandits on the neighbourhood, banging on the doors of every dwelling and issuing the 'trick or treat' challenge. Those evenings had always ended at the cottage, where they would arrive as late as they dared, flushed with fun, to warm themselves in Becky's kitchen and sip hot lemon with a tiny dash of rum, and pretend that they were getting roaring drunk.

Today, she had her doubts. 'But what about Ben?'

'I'm talking about Ben. We dress up and frighten the Mangles.'

'That'd take some doing. Sam, dearest, you don't

know the half of it, she thought.

'OK, then – we go to the cottage.'

'And then what?'

'Keep watch.'

'Until…?'

'Until the Mangles go out.'

'How d'you know the Mangles are going out?'

'You said they were. You said there was something important happening tonight.'

'Don't mean they're going out. Could be something happening *in* the cottage.' But she knew that wasn't true.

He didn't respond.

Gwynedd found silences hard to deal with. 'Tell me what you're thinking.' Whatever it was, it was best to get these things out in the open.

'What was your dad like?' he said.

She had never seen the absence of their dads as something they shared. To her, it had always been that she had no parents, whereas he had Becky. That was the crucial difference. But it was the death of his dad that had brought Sam to Rhayader in the first place, and maybe coming back was making him think about that.

'I dunno,' she said. 'Careless. Bit of a tearaway. Stupid. Didn't recognise a pearl when it was right under his nose.'

'A pearl? A real one? Valuable?'

'Me.' She smiled. 'I was a lovely baby. Dave said there was a photo of ma and dad holding me up for the camera when I was just a few days old. He can't find it now, of course. Pity, 'cos he says they were both smiling in the photo. Don't ever remember them smiling.' The image of her sitting in a field with a lamb on her lap came into her mind. 'I remember the rows and the unhappiness – fights, too.'

'Where did they go?'

'I dunno.'

'Why did they go?'

'Because they gave up.' She was suddenly angry. 'And that's why we're not gonna give up. Swear to me that we're not gonna give up.'

'Give up what?' said Sam.

'I dunno! Everything. Ben. Us. Meeting…seeing each other…writing letters…just – us.' What had started as almost a game, about a dog she hadn't really cared for, had somehow become the most important thing in her life. 'Don't go any further away than Bristol. I'd hate that. Swear to me you won't go any further away than Bristol.'

'How can I do that?' protested Sam. 'I don't know what's going to happen. I'm not the one who decides. Becky may get another job somewhere else.'

'I'm not talking about your blooming ma. I'm talking about you. About when… about later… when we're out of this childhood, teenage, stupid business. When *we* do the choosing. Swear you won't *choose* to go any further away than Bristol.'

She worked hard at him, but couldn't make him swear. She felt bitterly disappointed. In a couple of days he'd be back in Bristol, ninety-seven miles away, and Dave and Horseface might well be shipping her off to some bloomin' home. What use would being best mates be then?

CHAPTER 15

It was half past eight when they left the bungalow. Gwynedd had told Dave that she and Sam were going into town to meet up with old school mates and celebrate Halloween. Sam was impressed. He had forgotten how good Gwynedd was at telling lies. Dave had swallowed this one whole. Outside the bungalow, Sam and Gwynedd stood laughing together while he took more photographs of them with his fancy phone.

It was dark, it was cold, but they were warmly wrapped up. Sam was wearing a thick sweater under his posh jacket. Gwynedd had two sweaters and two T shirts. The added bulk made her feel bolder. They were going to do something at last, and she set off in a mood of high excitement. The terror of yesterday, when she was on her own in the woods, had disappeared in the joy of being out for a lark with Sam. She felt like a little kid. This might well be one last burst of freedom before Horseface had her way and stuck her in some shitty kids' home with a load of nosey old biddies spying on everything she did. If this was to be the end, at least she'd go out with a bang.

Keeping to the edge of the lane, they reached the bend before the cottage.

'This'll do,' said Gwynedd. 'Torch off.'

They ran down the field to the coppice at the bottom of Sam's old garden. Once in the trees, they worked their way along the stream.

'How about we plaster mud over our faces,' he said. Then he laughed. 'Not that you need it.'

He was right. There had been little enough point in smearing her own ugly mug with mushy peas when she went out to the Mangles' camp in broad daylight. Right now it was good and dark, and there was no need for mud to hide her skin, but wet mud was an irresistible plaything.

'So why don't I just help you do yours...'

She seized a large handful of cold sludge from the bottom of the stream and slapped it on his face.

'Bitch!'

'Let's just make sure I get your neck...'

Sam gave as good as he got, and by the time they were finished, both had hands and faces plastered with mud, and rivulets of cold and dirty water trickling down their bodies. She flashed a grin at him. He smiled back at her.

They crossed the stream, Sam leading, and she saw, in the light of the moon, his footprint in the wet mud at the water's edge. Her mind went back to another footprint, back in the summer... the night she had moved the stepping stone and he'd fallen in the stream... the night someone had run from the cottage. She shook her head. It seemed incredible to her that she'd never made any attempt to find out who it was.

Sam carefully wiped his hands clean on the damp grass.

'Fusspot,' she said.

'Give your mouth a rest.'

She laughed. Inside the smart new jacket, now looking a little the worse for wear, was the same old Sam.

He led the way through the trees at the side of the garden until they were some fifteen metres from the front of the cottage. From here, they could see the passage to the side of the building, the porch at the front, the short path leading to the gate, and the lane beyond. There were lights in the cottage.

'Now what do we do?'

'Nothing till we see the Mangles leave,' he said.

'When will that be?'

'How should I know? You're the one that said they were going out tonight. You have got your mobile, haven't you?'

Shit, she thought, shit, shit, shit. But she couldn't bring herself to tell him what had happened in the woods. 'Don't be daft,' she said quickly. 'Course I have.'

'Switched on?'

'Course it's switched on.'

'Well, switch it off, for God's sake! If that thing rings, it'll give us away.'

'Don't see much point in having it, if it's not switched on.'

'It's in case we get separated.' Sam made no attempt to keep the sarcasm out of his voice.

It was her turn to be sarcastic. 'Don't see who's going to separate us tonight. Unless you've a fancy to link up with that cow Mollie Pryce.' She turned her back on him, and pretended that she was fiddling with a mobile. 'All done,' she said.

For a while they said nothing. It occurred to Gwynedd that, if the Mangles really were planning to stage some sinister event tonight, she hadn't the slightest idea what time it might start. Late, presumably, long after honest folk were in bed and there was no chance of discovery. She recalled Len's words into his mobile, that night back in the summer, when she had hidden behind the water butt. "Friday... half past". Maybe tonight would also start at half past. But half past what?

'What time is it?' she said.

Sam switched his mobile on, shielding its glow with his hand. 'Twenty past nine.'

'We might have to wait hours.'

'I don't care.'

Her grubby brown hand reached out for his posh pink one.

The long wait began. Unpleasant thoughts began to niggle at her brain. She hadn't told Sam anything like the whole truth, hadn't told him what she reckoned the Mangles had planned for the night ahead. Sam thought they were simply snatching Ben from a bad home, like social services taking an abused kid into care. It was much more than that. It was a matter of life or death. She was pretty sure the Mangles were going to use Ben as a sacrifice to whip up the blood lust of Prince or Beauty before one of them was matched against another killer dog in a fight. Right now, Sam didn't know anything about this.

She felt decidedly uneasy. Ever since she had first met the Mangles, life had slipped further and further out of her control. She didn't like having to admit that she was frightened of the Mangles. More than that, she was also frightened by the knowledge that, at some point in the next few hours, Sam might well discover what was really going on. He'd have to know. She'd have to tell him, and take care of him afterwards. His poshness and his Spanish lessons and his taxi-money and his iPods wouldn't help him tonight, not one bit. This was real life. Welcome to the World of Survival. Right now, it was just a matter of Ben's survival but, if things got out of hand, it might be a matter of the survival of all three of them.

So much had happened in the last few months. Back in the summer, they'd been kids. Now? She didn't know what she was. Sam seemed to be growing up all right, but he'd never been a real kid. That was what made him different from the rest, from Vinnie and Little Huwie and the others. Was that why she was here, out in the cold, risking her neck, and holding Sam's hand? It had started with Ben, because no dog deserved what the Mangles had lined up for him. But, until now, she'd never felt about Ben like Sam did. So what was it?

She waited for some inner voice to answer her question, to butt in and say 'Do this, girl...' or 'Do that, girl...' But the inner voice didn't say anything. The inner voice had gone. And it never even bothered to say "goodbye". Just like ma and dad.

Sam withdrew his hand from her grasp.

'Got cramp,' he whispered.

She peered through the screen of trees. There was no sign of movement in the cottage. 'How much longer are we going to wait?'

'As long as it takes,' he said.

'What time is it now?'

'Nine thirty-five.'

Gwynedd was having second thoughts. 'We could go back to the bungalow,' she said. 'Come back for Ben tomorrow. Maybe early in the morning. Grab him when they let him out for a run.'

'We stay here till I get my dog.'

'You go on and on about Ben like he was still your dog. But he ain't. He's *theirs*. They can do what they want with him.'

'That's why we've got to get him back tonight,' said Sam.

There was a moment's silence, then Sam said: 'What do you mean... "do what they want with him"?'

'Nothing,' she said.

'What can they do to him?'

It was the hardest thing she'd ever done in her life.

172

She made a mess of it at first, but once she'd started, she knew she had to finish, and the words poured out. She said nothing of the loss of her mobile, aware that it was a dangerous subject. A part of her still blamed Sam for his call that had led to her discovery by the Mangles. But she told him about Dave and the dog-fights of long ago, about her fear that this was what the Mangles had planned for tonight. And as she told him, she finally faced up to the enormity of the task before them. When she finished, she felt years older than when she started.

'What's this got to do with Ben?'

He hadn't managed to take it all in.

'He may be involved.' She repeated some of the worst bits, going through what she thought was scheduled for that night. She'd expected Sam to explode – into action or tears, she wasn't sure which. She had her arms ready to grab him or hug him. But at first he said nothing, did nothing.

Eventually, he said: 'But Ben's no fighter.'

She had to see it through to the bitter end. She was about to take the plunge and tell him about the 'warm-up' victims, the dogs sacrificed to give the killers a taste of blood, when they saw headlights coming up the lane. It was the SUV.

The vehicle stopped, and Gwynedd recognised Len and the small man who'd been at the camp yesterday, when Prince had been weighed. Mags joined them from the cottage. The three talked, loudly enough for Gwynedd and Sam to pick up scraps of their hurried conversation. There was mention of "Level Fawr" and "Mitchell's Adit", of "look-outs" and "the main event".

Mags went back into the cottage, but reappeared almost immediately, carrying a pair of shotguns. She loaded them into the back of the SUV.

Gwynedd had already witnessed the vicious side of the Mangles, but for Sam the guns were a terrifying revelation.

'Right,' he said, much too loudly for safety. 'We get the police.'

'We can't!' She put as much power into the whisper as she could.

He started to move away, back towards the stream.

'Sam, wait!'

He was going. She couldn't stop him. The whole plan was going to come to nothing, just one big mess.

From somewhere near the SUV came a single frightened bark. It was enough. Sam froze.

'That's Ben,' he said. 'I'm going to get him.'

She grabbed the sleeve of his jacket. 'You'll get killed. They've got guns there, and they'll use them. Listen to me – I think I know where they're going. It's in the mountains.' She took a deep breath. 'That's where they're gonna have the dog-fight.'

He struggled. 'Let go!'

She tightened her grip on his sleeve, bracing herself to hold him back. 'No, Sam, no! You can't!'

The lights went out in the cottage. The front door slammed and Mags came hurrying down the path. She was clad in jeans, a thick anorak and heavy boots.

'Please, Sam!' hissed Gwynedd. She put her arms around him.

Mags slammed the rear door of the SUV shut.

Sam shook her off. 'I've got to get Ben!'

In a second, he would have been away from her, crashing through the hedge to get to his beloved dog, but the headlights of another vehicle flooded the lane with light, and a large white van drew up beside the SUV. Two men got out. Sam checked himself. He couldn't take on that many.

The two men were asking for directions. Mags pointed up the lane, and Gwynedd heard her repeat the words 'Level Fawr'. The words clearly meant nothing to their visitors. Mags and Len led them up the path to the cottage. Gwynedd heard Les saying 'there's a map inside'.

Sam put his head close and whispered in Gwynedd's ear. 'What's Level Fawr?'

'It's the name they give to part of the old lead mine at Cwmystwyth,' she whispered back. 'On the old road to Devil's Bridge. That's gotta be where they're holding the fights.'

'Quick,' said Sam. 'While they're all inside, we can get Ben.'

They scrambled out into the lane. Sam grabbed the handle on the rear door of the SUV and jiggled it up and down, but it was locked. He peered in and could see the crate that held his dog. Worse, Ben could see him, and the dog began whimpering plaintively.

'Smash it! Smash it open!' Sam looked desperately

around for a rock, a brick, a stone – anything that would break the glass of the door that separated him from Ben.

'It's no good,' said Gwynedd. 'It'd take ages, and they'll be out in a minute.' She looked swiftly about her. 'There's only one thing for it...the van...get in the back of the van. The other one! It's got to be going to the fight, and we'll go, too.' She dragged Sam to the back of the van and twisted the handle of the back doors. It turned. She flung one door open and leapt in. Sam followed, closing the door behind him.

There was just time for them to squeeze themselves behind some large metal drums – like overgrown paint tins – before they heard footsteps on the gravel path. The front doors were wrenched open and the van shifted as the men flopped into the front seats. They heard one of the men say: 'OK. Len says straight up the lane and keep going. Ten miles, he said. When we get near, we flash the headlights three times for the signal.'

The engine started. The van lurched forward. The metal drums swayed and shifted, threatening to pin Sam and Gwynedd against the sides of the van or crash down on them. They drew close together. The van accelerated, beginning the long and tortuous climb into the heart of the mountains. The roar of its engine and the rattle of its cargo made enough noise to drown the whispered conversation between Sam and Gwynedd.

'I was right,' she said. 'We're heading for the old mine at Cwmystwyth.'

'What happens there?'

'We get our last chance to save Ben.'

CHAPTER 16

Once upon a time the old lead mine at Cwmystwyth had been a place of employment and industry, of noise and sweat – a place where over a hundred men scratched their way into the dark mountain to strip the metal ore from its hard heart. It had been a tough way to earn a living, but it had supported an entire community. In those days there had been houses and offices, stables and a blacksmith's forge, a tramway and a weighbridge. There had been a large, iron-spoked waterwheel powering the machine that pumped water out of the mines, and a gaunt barracks block to house the miners who worked there. The men spent their days digging and blasting the lead-bearing ore, and their nights singing and talking together, but drinking little, for they were Methodists. The broken lumps of rock hacked from the hillside were shovelled on to conveyor belts and sent to the great crushing mill. And, in that once upon a time, this was where the noise had been at its most deafening, as machines hammered mountain rocks into manageable pieces of stone, from which the precious ore could be extracted.

But the deafening noise had long ceased to echo back and forth across the narrow valley. All that could be heard now was the moaning of the wind blowing through what was left of the mine buildings. The old waterwheel had rusted into a locked position and would never turn again. The mine-shafts and tunnels were all closed. A century of storms had torn the conveyor belt to ribbons. Only the outer walls of the barracks block remained. The old smithy had no roof. The sole surviving building was the crushing mill. It was large, three storeys high, each storey shorter and narrower than the one below it, so it tapered upwards like a three tier wedding cake. Its roofs and walls were built of hundreds of sheets of corrugated iron fastened to a steel framework. The sheets glowed with rust, and through them peered glass-less windows. The whole compound had long been still and silent. It was like an abandoned fort in a desert wasteland, defended by only a ghostly garrison.

Around the front and sides of the crushing mill lay vast piles of shale. What had been part of the mountain body for millions of years was condemned to spend the rest of its existence as little more than heaps of stones. But the piles of shale shielded some of the old mill from the worst of the Welsh elements, and were about to provide cover for some strange and grim activities.

Behind the mill were the mountains, steep sided, thinly coated with the short grass that the sheep kept in trim, and flecked here and there with the occasional wizened tree and patch of bare rock. In front of the mill was the road from Rhayader to Devil's Bridge – not as old as the mountains, but old enough to have known the weight of ancient warriors, of pack-horses and oxen, of cattle shuffling through on the first leg of a journey from the pastures of Wales to the death-houses of the London meat markets. It had known the feet of tramps and thieves, monks and poachers, and the wheels of carts and solid-tyred bicycles, of early automobiles and modern SUVs.

There was scant traffic on the road tonight. Len and Mags had invited a couple of dozen carefully selected guests to their evening's entertainment in the roofless smithy. A few cars and a couple of vans were already parked well off the road, hidden by the largest of the heaps of shale. Inside the smithy, by the light of hurricane lamps, men were constructing a small arena in which the dogs would fight. The sides of it were made from old doors, bits of railing, and bales of hay. The men worked quickly and quietly, with sentries posted a couple of hundred metres along the road – in both directions – to give warning of the approach of any police car or trouble-maker.

The sentry on the Rhayader side of the mine saw the lights of the van carrying Sam and Gwynedd before it crossed the little stone bridge over the Afon Ystwyth, a mile away. Half a mile nearer, the van lights flashed off and on three times, and the sentry relaxed. The van drove slowly past him and turned off the road. It pulled up beside the other vehicles, by the heap of stones. The driver and his mate left the van. They walked across the yard to the smithy and joined the others working on the completion of the arena.

There were no windows in the back or sides of the van. Gwynedd and Sam could see nothing, but Gwynedd sensed that they had arrived at the old mine. The first problem was getting out of the van, for there was no handle on the inside of the rear doors. Sam ran his hand along the groove where the doors met. There was a pair of bolts running from both the roof and the floor of the van to the catch in the middle, which was operated by the door handle on the outside. He tugged first at the top, then the bottom. The bolt didn't budge.

'It's the handle. I can't make the handle turn from the inside. We'll have to break it open. We've got to get out before the men come back.'

In the darkness of the back of the van, they searched through the jumble with their hands, until they found a large, badly chipped chisel. Using this as a lever, they bent the bolt, forcing it out of the catches at floor and roof level. It was then a simple matter to push the back doors open and make their escape.

They slipped across the yard, heading for the nearest heap of shale. Once they were safely behind it, they risked peeping out to take stock of their position. Beyond the grim outline of the crushing mill they could see the glow of faint light coming from the smithy. It wasn't difficult to guess that this was where the fight would be staged. As yet, there was no sign of the Mangles' SUV.

'What time is it?' asked Gwynedd.

Sam unzipped his jacket pocket and took out his flash mobile. 'Gone eleven.'

'Dave'll have to get his own night-cap tonight.'

'We have to call the police.'

'It's no good. Dave says they're part of this whole dog-fight business. We're on our own, Sam.' It was too dark for her to be able to see how he reacted to this news. 'Switch it off,' she said. It would be too much to be betrayed on successive days by a mobile.

'Done that.' He shoved the mobile back in his pocket. 'Suppose the Mangles don't bring Ben here? Suppose they're taking him somewhere else?'

'It's gotta be here,' said Gwynedd. 'The lights in that old stone hut, and these blokes here at this hour of night.'

He plucked at her sleeve. 'See the roof of that big building?' He pointed to the crushing mill. 'We'd see what was going on all right from the top of that.'

He was right. 'Follow me.' She dashed out from behind the stones and across the yard, keeping the mill between her and the smithy. Sam hurried after her. Seconds later they were inside the mill, breathlessly gulping in the cold night air, and gazing up at what was left of the floors above.

'Up there.'

'It's dangerous.'

'Not if we're quick,' said Gwynedd.

'And careful.' He glanced at her. There was almost a full moon, and by its light he could see excitement in her eyes. She was actually enjoying all this. She loved it – the danger, the terror, the risks, the lateness of the hour, the madness of their situation. And it really was mad. Even if they rescued Ben, they would then have to find their own way home across miles of desolate mountain, almost certainly with the Mangles chasing after them. And the Mangles had two sets of lethal weapons – guns and dogs. For the first time since he had moved, Sam saw the attraction of the flat in Bristol.

'Think what a tale you'll have to tell your girlfriends when you get back to Bristol,' she said.

'Three things,' he said. 'One - this is for Ben. Two - I haven't got any girlfriends. Three - the way things are looking right now, I may not get back to Bristol...'

'Good,' she said. 'Let's go.'

They flitted from one metal pillar to another, looking for some kind of stairway or a ladder up to the next floor. Flurries of wind whipped through the mill, whistling as they filtered their way between the sheets of corrugated iron. Sam and Gwynedd trod carefully, avoiding the puddles, the chippings of rock and the twisted fragments of metal that littered the ground. All the time, they were coming nearer to the light that flickered from the lamps in the old smithy.

Sam stopped and pointed. He'd seen a possible route upwards. A section of the mill had collapsed, and a couple of drunkenly leaning pillars formed a kind of ramp leading at an angle of forty-five degrees to the middle storey of the mill. 'Maybe over there. Maybe we can find a way on to the roof.'

Gwynedd led the way to the ramp, and began to climb, moving lightly on all fours. At the top she gingerly tested what was left of the floor, to make sure it was strong enough to bear their weight. She looked back. Sam was doing his best to catch up with her, but his progress was slower and noisier. She wanted to call out to him, encourage him, nip back to help him. But negotiating the ramp was a job for one at a time. She watched his stuttering progress, as he stretched his hands out in front of him, gripped the edge of the ramp, and then slithered the rest of his body forward a little at a time. It was tricky work, but in a couple of minutes he had joined her, some five metres above the puddles and debris below.

She wasted no time, but moved onwards and upwards, climbing another few metres before she looked back. What the hell was he doing? No, don't be stupid, Sam. Don't go testing your bloody torch to see if it still works. It's too weak to be of any use, but bright enough to give us away.

'Switch it off! They'll see us!' she hissed at him.

She squeezed between two sheets of iron, shuffled her way along a girder, and hauled herself out on to the lower section of the roof. Now was the time to coax Sam from the relative safety of the first floor to join her in a more dangerous and exposed position. She made a funnel with her hands, and issued a series of hoarsely whispered instructions. Urgency and fear led to confusion: her "left" was Sam's "right", her "down" was his "up", her "this way" was Sam's "that way". Further time was wasted in a whispered argument. Like we were a bloomin' married couple, she thought, and for a moment wanted to laugh. Eventually he reached her.

She wanted to praise him. 'My darling Sam...'

'Just leave it.'

They had climbed to more than fifteen metres above ground, perched on the very top of the crushing mill, doing their best to protect themselves from the wickedly jagged edges of the corrugated iron, and peering down into the smithy. It was a perilous position but, as she had predicted, an excellent look-out post.

The fighting circle was complete. Half a dozen men stood around, drinking from cans, smoking, chatting and occasionally swaggering across to admire and to bait a solidly built dog kept under strict and savage control by its owner. Gwynedd shuddered at the thought of what a dog like that could do to Ben.

'Are you cold?'

'No.' It was true. She wasn't cold. She was scared.

'You must be.' He put his arm round her.

Reluctantly, she pushed it away. 'You'll have us both over the edge. And I'm not a baby.'

'You don't have to be so bloody touchy. You don't have to stay. I can do this on my own.'

Nerves were raw. They were both frightened, but Gwynedd's fear was laced with anger. She twisted round to face him and give him an earful, but as she did, she saw over his shoulder, way up the valley...near the little bridge over the river...there, the headlights of a vehicle flickering through the trees that grew by the waterside. They crouched down again. Things would change once the Mangles arrived.

The SUV slowed as it passed the crushing mill, and drew up by the smithy. A welcoming committee left the arena and crossed over to the vehicle. There were handshakes, and one of the men planted a smacking kiss on Mags's lips.

'Yuk!' muttered Gwynedd. 'And to think, she fancies you.'

'Just shut your face,' Sam said quietly. He'd told her to do that so often in the past. It made her feel better.

Len unlocked the back of the SUV, passed one crate to Mags, and then slowly eased out another crate that was clearly much heavier. The crates were taken into the smithy, where there were more handshakes. There was a round of hard talking, and the exchange of three or four packets, each about the size of a brick.

'Drugs,' said Sam.

Gwynedd was impressed. 'Who's a smart city boy, then?' she whispered.

But as the men opened the packets, she could see that they were stuffed not with drugs, but with money, a lot of money. Dozens of notes were counted into the hands of two men with camera and tripod.

'What's that?'

'They're going to film the fight,' said Sam. 'Put it on the Net. Stick it on DVDs. Maybe get a lot of money from people sick enough to watch that sort of stuff.' He had made up his mind. All he wanted to do was find Ben and get him out of there, no matter what it cost. But the rescue couldn't start until Ben appeared. Where the hell was he?

Gwynedd's thoughts were ahead of him. She guessed the dog was in one of the crates far below, perhaps the one that she had seen Mags drag to the edge of the makeshift arena. She was better prepared than Sam for what happened next.

Mags stood the crate on a bale of straw, opened it, and tipped out the contents.

The contents were Ben, who staggered to his feet, tail between his quivering legs. He made no attempt to escape, but stood in the middle of the circle, with his head down. The onlookers gathered round, mocking the dog. The shrill voice of Mags was loud enough to cut through the night air to reach the ears of Sam and Gwynedd.

'Bye-bye, Bennikins. I won't say it hasn't been nice knowing you, but as a matter of fact, it hasn't.'

The mocking increased. Len was bending over the other crate. He must have said something to goad the dog inside this one, for there was a furious burst of snarling from within.

'Come on, Prince.' Len's voice came to them clearly. He was shouting above the snarling, and he was showing off. 'My lords, ladies and gentlemen... a little treat for you tonight... a little appetiser to get the evening under way...'

The crowd leaned forward. It was time to see what they were going to get for their money tonight.

Sam and Gwynedd watched in horror as Len's hand

moved to his pocket, feeling for the padlock key to open the crate. But the key wasn't there... not that pocket... must be the other one... no... must have left it in the dashboard.

'Get a move on, Len. Don't keep us hanging about.'

'Slight delay, ladies and gents. Back in a tick...'

CHAPTER 17

'Trust me.'

'What are you going to do?'

'Just trust me,' she said. 'And do what I do.' She had it all sorted in her mind. It was best to make the whole thing sound like a playground game, like they were back together in the Juniors, or in the playground in the park. 'This way...'

She set off in a monkey run along the very top of the roof, feet and hands straddling the ridge. She moved fast, too fast for Sam. She left him behind, but this was a desperate situation. He'd have to do the best he could. Once they'd snatched the dog, maybe they could leg it up the road, find a passing car and beg a lift, or seek sanctuary at some remote farmhouse. Something had to be done. The dog would be dead in a minute.

She reached the far end of the ridge, and looked back. Where was Sam? He'd hardly moved. What was it? Lost his nerve? Then they'd had it... no, wait... good boy, good boy... He was moving. Thank God. But what was he doing? She shoved her fist in her mouth to stifle a scream.

Sam was lying on his back, and slithering feet first down the far side of the roof, out of sight of Len, Mags and all the others. Stupidly, he had chosen the quickest, but the noisiest and most dangerous route to the ground. His sliding body moved faster and faster, completely out of control, until his feet hit the guttering at the bottom of the upper roof, and checked his fall. The impact tore the metal strip from its ancient fastenings. The guttering rolled and bounced down the lower roof, clattering and clanging over the corrugated iron, and plummeting down to the yard below with a crash that reverberated through the mill.

The noise and the shock threw Gwynedd off balance, but she managed to anchor her body across the ridge of the roof. Her first, sickening thought was that Sam had followed the guttering over the edge, his body smashing on the yard below. She had to know. She had to see.

She slithered down one of the pitched girders that supported the roof end until she reached a point from which she could look down. Thank God... he hadn't gone over the edge. Along the top of the mill wall there was a row of windows with heavy metal frames. The frames jutted out from under the eaves of the roof, and Sam's feet had lodged in the top of one of the frames. This had stopped his fall. She could imagine the jarring, bruising jolt he must have felt through his whole body when this happened. It was a wonder he hadn't broken his back, but the light of the moon was strong enough for her to see that he was slowly recovering, slowly moving to a safer position. As he did so, his flash mobile slipped from the unzipped pocket of his fancy bloody jacket, and disappeared over the edge of the roof. She heard the crack as it hit the ground.

The clattering and banging on the roof had set the dogs barking and halted the fun and games in the smithy. Dog-masters and spectators had left the smithy and hurried out into the yard. One of the men flashed the beam of a powerful torch over the mill.

'Switch it off, you bloody fool,' shouted another. 'A light like that could be seen miles away.'

'What's up, Babe?' Len's voice came from behind one of the vans.

Then there was another shout, from the same place. 'For Chrissake, Mags, tell your husband to put that gun away!'

'How about it, Mags? Keep it handy...just in case? So's I can protect you.' He was by the SUV, with the padlock key at last in his hand.

'That's why I love him so,' said Mags. 'A gentleman in a crisis. You won't find many of them these days.'

Len gave orders to the men. 'Spread out round the old building,' he said. 'Surround it. Let's have a look, see what's going on.' A couple of them moved to his command, but most were reluctant. The sudden interruption to the night's entertainment had unnerved some of the weaker hearted.

'Somebody shut those dogs up!'

'Tell me how...'

'We'll have the whole of Wales up here in a minute...'

While this exchange was taking place, Sam had managed to twist his body round into a position from which he could jump on to the lower roof. He bent his knees and leapt, landing safely, but making more noise. Gwynedd's spirits recovered. To be able to jump like that, he must be OK.

'Other side, like I said!' shouted Len. 'There's someone there.' Boots crunched across the yard, but some were heading towards the vehicles parked behind the heaps of shale.

A voice called out: 'You're on your own with this one, Len. If you let fly with that shotgun at some copper or a bloody RSPCA snooper, we'll all end up in jail.'

'What about you, Nash?' Len shouted back. 'You with me, or what?'

'Sorry, Len, no can do. I've got my dog to consider. And let's give things time to settle down before we fix a rematch, eh?'

There were the sounds of vehicle doors opening, of crates being flung inside, of dogs barking and men shouting, of slamming doors. A moment later half a dozen cars and vans pulled out from behind the pile of stones, to head down the road towards Devil's Bridge.

Len took charge. 'The rest of you stay put. If Nash hasn't got the guts to see this thing through, that's his bad luck. I promised you blood tonight, and blood is what you'll get... though where the blood'll come from, I'm not sure... yet.'

Gwynedd knew that if she and Sam were to have

any chance of escape, they must move now, and move fast. She reached the ground, and looked round for somewhere to hide. There... in the corner, at the far end of the mill, furthest from the old smithy. It was pitch dark there... if they could get to that corner without being seen... She sprinted the length of the mill and had just enough time to cram her body into a gap between two girders before the first of the departing cars accelerated past her. The vans followed. Right, with that lot gone there were fewer blokes left to help the Mangles in their search. The odds had shortened. Gwynedd reckoned they were down to about six-to-one, and the mill was a big place. More to the point, if she and Sam could slip away unseen, up the steep mountainside at the back of the mill, they'd take some finding, for the mountains rolled back many a mile, and there were no roads along which vehicles could pursue them.

But where was Sam now?

She risked sneaking out from her hiding place to take a look. Was that him? At the other end... twenty metres away? Yeah... but what the hell was he doing? She didn't dare call out, but beckoned furiously to him. It was useless. He was moving away from her, towards the smithy, towards danger. Then she heard his voice, at full pitch, calling his poor, stupid dog.

'Ben! Ben! Here, Ben!'

It had been eight weeks since the ears, that instantly pricked up, had heard that voice, but, with memory refreshed by the glimpse of Sam at the SUV's window half an hour ago, Ben recognised the call at once. The dog scrambled over the planks and bales of straw, belted out of the smithy and raced across the yard.

Len, too, recognised the voice. 'It's that lovely young Sam,' he said, and he mimicked Sam's voice. 'Here, Sam!' he shouted. 'Here, boy!' As he called, he pulled back the catches on the shotgun.

'No games, Len. Those bloody kids could have us put away.'

'I'm not playing games, Babe.' Len's voice changed to an angry roar. 'And I'll blow little Bennikins away if you kids don't come out...now!'

Gwynedd had no way of knowing how real the threat was. But then she saw a dog – it had to be Ben – cavorting round Sam's legs at the far end of the dark mill. She could just make out Sam trying to pat the dog while he looked round for an escape route. She saw Sam suddenly stop. He must have heard something. Then she heard it – shuffling feet moving round the outside of the dilapidated building – and she knew that the hunters had spread out so that they covered all sides. The place was surrounded.

The light of the moon was stronger now, lighting up the entire compound and penetrating large sections of the mill itself. She could see Sam clearly, twisting his head this way and that, while his bloody feet were firmly rooted to the ground. And if she could see Sam, you could bet what was left of your life that it wouldn't be long before other eyes spotted him.

She had to risk it. She left her hiding place to dash

towards him, and in so doing, banged into one of the metal sheets hanging from the wall. It crashed to the ground. Sam whirled round, dropped to his knees, shielding Ben with his own body.

'Don't.'

He was begging.

She realised that he had no idea who she was. The last voices he had heard had been those of the Mangles, so he assumed that the figure racing towards him was either the mad woman or the brute with the gun. He was trying to protect his dog from slaughter.

'Sam! This way!'

She veered to the side and headed out into the yard, with Sam scrambling after her and Ben leaping at his side. Once clear of the mill, she made for the largest heap of stones, a mountain of shale piled against the great wall of rock where the mountain had been blasted away to make room for the mine buildings.

'Up here!' She plunged on to the pile of stones and began climbing. Ben raced ahead of her, Sam struggled in her wake. She heard footsteps pounding across the yard below.

It was a nightmare chase, for both she and Sam found their feet slipping and sliding as they struggled to get a grip on the shifting surface of the loose stones. For all their efforts, she felt as though they were making snail-like progress in a kind of heavily drugged slow motion, while their pursuers were racing across the yard at full speed. She glanced over her shoulder. Good, good! The climb was tough enough for her and Sam, but virtually impossible for the men chasing them. They were heavier, far less fit, and in some cases considerably the worse for drink. They could barely keep their balance, sinking to their ankles in the shifting stones, and crunching back two steps for every two steps they took forward.

She reached the top of the heap and turned to face them. They were still near the bottom, with a monstrous pile to climb. Sam was more than halfway up, but in need of help. She filled her hands with lumps of stone from the pile. In other circumstances it was the sort of thing she would have enjoyed. She knew how to throw, and if she'd had time to take careful aim, she could have done considerable damage. But right now the object was to worry them, hassle them, throw them off balance, rather than knock their teeth out. She flung the stones two or three at a time, a stinging fusillade that made the men duck and raise their arms to ward off the missiles. It bought Sam precious time to struggle on.

But Len was not in the mood for games. He was standing at the foot of the stones, shotgun in hand. He shouted to the men struggling in front of him to get out of the way. Then he raised the gun to his shoulder and aimed it at Sam. 'Now then, Sammy,' he said. 'Down you come.' And he called up to Gwynedd. 'Drop those stones, you interfering little tart, or your boyfriend will never walk again.'

Mags joined him. 'I should do as Len says,' she called up. 'He's got this thing about guns. Loves firing them.

Makes him feel he's a real man.'

'I'll show you who's a real bloody man.' Len's voice rang round the yard.

'That'll be the day,' said Mags.

'Your Len's bloody mad.'

Gwynedd recognised the voice as that of the driver of the van she and Sam had hidden in.

'And we'd be mad to get caught up in this. Nash was right. We could all get banged up for this one.' The driver slithered down the shale, shoved his way past Len and made for his van. His mate followed him.

Len swore at their retreating backs and turned on the remaining men. 'What about you lot? Staying or going?'

'Well, you see, Len, ...it's like this... No offence, or anything. You're a good enough bloke and we all think the world of your lady wife...'

Mags swivelled round. She spat on the ground and snatched the gun from Len. 'Get out of here,' she snarled. 'You bunch of scum! Cowards, the lot of you.'

The attention of Len and Mags was fully occupied by the ill-tempered spat taking place below. Just for a moment, the barrels of the gun no longer threatened Sam. Gwynedd leant forward, urging Sam to scrabble up the last few metres of the shale pile. 'Come on, Sam. If we can just make it to that bit of rock...'

There was a gap between the top of the pile, where she was standing, and an outcrop of rock jutting through the fringe of the turf. It was not even two metres wide, but the loose stones beneath her feet gave her little purchase for the jump, no solid base from which to take off. If she missed her footing, she would fall between the rock-face and the stones, and there would be nothing to stop her slithering down until her body became trapped between the two. No point in waiting though. The gap wasn't going to get any smaller. She hurled herself forward and grabbed the exposed roots of a stunted rowan tree. The roots tore from the soil. Earth and stones fell into her face. She grabbed another root, stronger, more deeply embedded in the soil, and hauled herself on to the flat rock. For the moment, she was safe, but the force of her jump had dislodged an avalanche of shale from the top of the pile. It rolled down towards Sam and swept him off balance. As he toppled over, more shale shifted beneath his feet, and she watched in horror as he began to slide towards the ground.

'Gwynedd!'

It was a return to slow motion terror. At times he looked to have regained his balance, halted his slide. But, as soon as he tried climbing again, the stones rattled and rolled from under him, and he stumbled and fell back once more. Beyond his staggering body, Gwynedd could see the Mangles, staring up at Sam. There was a twisted smile on the face of Mags, as though she was enjoying Sam's pathetic attempts to recover, to climb, to escape. The woman stood the butt of her gun on the ground. There was now no need for firearms. She blew Sam a kiss, and beckoned to him, encouraging his fall. Len and a couple of his mates moved forward, planting their feet firmly on the bottom of the pile, ready to grab Sam as soon as he was within reach.

'Sam!'

Gwynedd knew her cry was useless. Sam was plunging nearer and nearer to capture. She could do nothing to prevent it. She watched his frantic efforts to anchor his feet in the shale, but the harder he struggled, the further he fell. He glanced helplessly up at her, and, through the tears that filled her eyes, she stared back. Sam was lost. All she could do was give up and make her way down to join him. There was no way she'd run off and leave him to it.

But there was one present who could do something. Ben had no difficulty keeping his balance on the sloping pile, no difficulty in moving up or down, and the dog could see Sam slipping away. Ben's paws rattled over the stones as he scurried down to Sam. In the dog's mind, in its memory, in its instinct was the old game, the old welcoming game that it had played every day when Sam came home from school. Without a word from Sam, the dog seized the sleeve of Sam's beautiful new jacket in its teeth, and braced its legs against the drag of his master's weight. Sam's body came to rest beyond the reach of the Mangles. While Ben tugged on one arm, Sam used his other arm and his feet to hoist himself slowly back up the pile. Stones clattered down, but Ben and Sam were moving steadily upwards.

Gwynedd wiped the tears from her face. 'Come on, Ben!' she shouted. 'Come on! Good dog!'

There were other shouts from the ground. Len had snatched the gun back. Once more he brought it up to his shoulder. 'You stop where you are, sonny. Or I will shoot. One cartridge may well do for you and Bennikins. If it doesn't...well, the other should finish off the pair of you.'

'Easy, Len,' said Mags, quietly, but the others round her were less calm.

'For Chrissake, Len...'

One of the men grabbed the barrel of the gun, seeking to wrestle it from Len's grasp. Len swung the butt of the shotgun into the pit of the man's stomach, winding him. The man grunted with pain, but held on until Len's free arm went round the man's neck and jerked him backwards so that he lost his grip on the gun. A second man flung himself on Len and the two crashed to the ground. The rest of the crowd quickly melted away, scurrying to their cars.

Sam and Ben reached the top of the pile.

'Here!' screamed Gwynedd. 'Jump here!' She could see Mags lashing out with her foot, helping Len drag himself free from the others. The gun was loose on the ground. Len was back on his feet, grabbing the gun.

Sam leapt, snatched at the tree roots, caught them, lost them and then felt his arm almost leave its socket as Gwynedd grabbed his wrist and hauled him on to the rock. There was a deafening explosion as the gun went off, but Len had fired too soon, and the pellets buried themselves harmlessly in the shale, well below the rock. Before he could fire the second barrel, the man Len had winded struggled back to his feet and knocked the gun from Len's hands.

The man kicked it out of reach and shouted to his mate. 'We're out of here...' The mate fought his way free of Mags's grasp and the two men followed the others, who were already driving off. Engines roared. Tyres screamed and smoked as all the remaining vehicles, save the SUV, accelerated out of the yard and on to the road. As the last car raced past, Len picked up the shotgun, steadying himself to fire at the windscreen.

Sam hurried away up the slope, taking Ben with him. Gwynedd didn't follow immediately. She flattened herself against the edge of the rock, mad with curiosity to know what would happen next. She saw Mags reach out her hand to take the gun from Len. Snatches of their conversation were blown up to Gwynedd, borne on the wind that spiralled round the amphitheatre created when the mine buildings were cut into the hillside.

'Forget them cowards, Len... it's the kids we want...'

Gwynedd saw Len take a deep breath.

'You're right, Babe...'

She saw Mags stab her finger towards the hillside. '...up there...'

Gwynedd wondered if it was just a guess, or whether Mags could actually see Sam as he stumbled round the screes of rock, making for the thick bracken that covered the lower slopes of the mountain. Once in there, the Mangles would never find them.

More words reached her.

'...back to the bridge. Tell... tonight's party is off... head for home...'

Were the Mangles leaving? Had they had enough?

It was Len who was doing most of the talking, searching through his pockets as he did so. '...lost children... anything might happen... over a precipice... reservoirs... bogs... dreadful things might happen...' He found the key at last. '... no need to worry... me and Beauty will find them...'

The dogs! Gwynedd had forgotten the dogs. No good hiding in bracken with dogs after you. Len wasn't giving up. It was time to go. She slithered backwards off the rock, staggered to her feet and sprinted after Sam.

The wind blew afresh, and brought a new sound to her ears... the baying of a hound.

CHAPTER 18

Sam wasn't hard to find. It was easy to trace his floundering route through the bracken from the bent stalks and trampled ferns he'd left behind him. When she caught up with him, Gwynedd couldn't see the anxiety on his face, but she could hear it clearly enough in his voice.

'What the hell have you been doing?'

'Just checking on what the Mangles will do next.'

'And?'

She wanted to say something reassuring. 'Sounds like they may be heading for home.'

'You wish. They won't give up now.'

She reckoned he was right. She just hadn't wanted to be the one to break the bad news.

'Hear that?' She grabbed Sam's hand. 'That's the SUV. They're off somewhere.'

They stood up, peering over the bracken tops, and saw a tiny pair of red lights, moving swiftly away along the road.

'Good,' said Sam. 'We can check where they're going

from their tail-lights.'

It was as though the Mangles had heard him. The lights were switched off and the black vehicle became invisible. Gwynedd guessed what they would do; drive half a mile or so up the valley, back towards Cwmystwyth, and then split up. Mags would drive on. Len and Beauty would get on to the hillside where the slope was gentler. If she and Sam followed their instinctive desire to leg it back to the bungalow, there was a real danger that they'd run slap into their pursuers. To avoid that risk, they'd have to make a wide detour.

'I don't care if the police are involved in these dog-fights,' said Sam. 'They can't turn a blind eye to murder. I'm calling them.' He put his hand in his pocket.

'It's not there,' said Gwynedd. 'It fell out when you slipped on the roof...'

'Mum'll kill me...'

'She'll have to wait her turn.'

'Use your mobile.'

'Already tried that. No good. No signal.' This was no time to own up to the previous lie.

'Bloody Wales!'

'Nothing wrong with Wales. It's your bloody dog.'

'Well? He's Welsh.'

Nor was this a good time to have a row. They'd better save their breath for the long march ahead. 'Don't let's hang about,' she said. 'We're off to Llangurig. It's a pretty walk.' And a rough one too, she thought. They'd have to cross that bog on Bryn Copra, skirt round the massive forest of Esgair Ychion, and pray that Beauty's tracking skills didn't match the brute's killing skills.

'Come on.'

She led the way through the bracken and out on to the open mountainside. Even Gwynedd had only the vaguest idea as to what direction they should take. She reckoned to the right, towards the east. They would have to climb first, get to the high ground. Once there, she hoped she'd be better able to read the landscape. She reckoned they needed to keep the forest to their left... Whatever happened, she knew they had to stay out of Esgair Ychion, an unbroken, twenty-five square mile fastness of fir-trees. In daylight it was easy enough to get lost there. In darkness, they wouldn't stand a chance. No, they must keep just below the skyline, and all the time make for the track that hugged the eastern edge of the forest. Eventually, please God, they would come to the little town of Llangurig, just a few miles north of Rhayader. If they could only reach the houses on the outskirts, they should be safe. Not even Len would dare set his dog on them where there were doors to beat on, windows to smash, and maybe passing cars. But Llangurig was more than ten punishing miles away, the night was cold, they were exhausted, and they had nothing to eat.

She was just about to pass on to Sam an edited version of her thoughts, when they both heard a snatch of deep-throated barking. They couldn't be sure where it came from, but it was not far away.

'That's Beauty,' she said. Ben was whimpering. She

felt like joining him. 'But we can move faster than that ugly brute with its tongue lolling out of its slobbering mouth.'

'That's no way to talk about Len,' said Sam. 'And don't worry about him. We'll leave that fat git miles behind.'

He made it sound like they were playing some virtual reality game. If only...

As they jogged along, Gwynedd tried to think ahead. The march had to be planned. It was no good racing off like it was a sprint through the campsite to catch the school bus. To be safe, they'd have to keep going for hours, across miles of rough country. And they had to keep a fair distance ahead of that brute of a dog. If it got sight of them, it'd charge in for the kill. There was a tough night ahead, but if they could make it to the Llangurig road, they might just be all right.

'When this is all over, we'll have a feast down at the chippie to celebrate.'

'Great,' said Sam. 'Ketchup's on me.'

She could sense he wanted to hurry. 'Remember that map Mr Richards painted in the corridor? In the Juniors? With all the villages on?' She wanted to slow him down. 'We've got bloody miles to go.'

They were steadily climbing. It was the obvious way to go, but Gwynedd had one reservation about her plan. It was *too* bloody obvious. Mags had a powerful brain in that nasty mind of hers. She'd been smart enough to turn out the lights on her posh bloody car. Like as not she'd also guessed the route that they were taking. So, how about the old drovers' track? The

Mangles weren't local. They mightn't know about that. Gwynedd tried to remember where the hell it went after it left the Rhayader road down by the bridge. Into the mountains, that was for sure, but it twisted and turned worse than a corkscrew, so where did it come out? At Llangurig? Or did it snake its way back to the Rhayader road, further down the steep valley? Or go up into the forest? Gwynedd found herself wishing she'd paid more attention to dear old, daft old Mr Richards and his huge-scale map.

They came to a narrow gully in the mountainside, where a stream juddered its way between rocks and boulders, lapping round the lower limbs of a few bent and grizzled trees, and bubbling into a series of small pools.

'What do we do?' said Sam. 'Keep going? This way?'

They moved cautiously down into the gully, leaning sideways into the slope, feeling about them for any tree roots, rocks or clumps of bracken that they could grasp to steady their descent. Their hands were cold and clumsy, and the scraping, burning touch of stone and wet stalks made their skin raw and painful. But they safely negotiated their way down to the junction of their stream with another. Here the water hurled itself over dark, slippery boulders. It was no place to attempt a crossing in the dark. They struggled back upstream. After some hard climbing, they came to a place where the gully widened and the land levelled out so that the fall of the water was less precipitous.

Sam took the lead. 'We don't just cross,' he said. 'We

have to wade along the stream as far as we can. So the dog has to keep searching the other bank to pick up our scent.'

'What about your flash trainers?'

'Bollocks to my flash trainers.' Sam set off, testing his footing at each step.

Well, she thought, Bristol ain't completely ruined him, then. Gwynedd followed him, treading where he had trodden, and swearing at Ben, for the dog kept splashing back to her, as though she needed its bloody assistance.

'Get off!'

Ben did as he was told, bounding out of the stream on to the far bank, and leaving his scent all over the place.

'Stupid, *stupid* animal.'

'He can't help it,' said Sam.

'So why don't you stop him? He's your dog.'

She lost her temper and her concentration. Her next step was ill-judged, and she fell forward, banging her knee on a sharp rock, and plunging her arms in the icy water.

'Shit!' She dragged herself upright and limped to the far bank. Her knee was agony and her pride was badly hurt.

'You all right?' said Sam.

'Yeah. I'm fine. I've just shattered my knee and torn the skin off my arm. I'm soaking wet, and cold to the bone. There's a murderer and a mad dog after us. We're miles from help. I'm fine. Everything's fine.'

It was all Sam's fault. If he hadn't gone to Bristol, none of this would have happened. *He* should have been the one to slip and end up in the water. He wasn't as fit as her. He wasn't as tough as her. These were *her* bloody mountains. This was *her* bloody stream. *He* should have been the one to fall over.

'Sorry, Gwynedd. But we have to keep going.' He held his hand out towards her.

'Leave me alone. I can manage.'

'OK. Just follow me, and look where you're going.'

He headed for the higher ground. She stuck her tongue out at him from behind his back.

They reached a plateau, where the dark mass of the forest stretched out in front of them. Here Gwynedd veered to the right, to the east, aiming to strike the edge of the forest a mile or so on. But it was hard work, slow going across bog and marsh, with feet sinking into puddles of peat-brown water. With each step, there was the danger of twisting a knee, breaking an ankle. Progress was slow, and hard, and painful. They were both in difficulties. He was panting heavily, grunting each time he had to find the extra strength to lift his foot from the sucking morass of the sticky bog, gasping with the effort of climbing over the clumps of grass. She saw him clutch his side, as though he had a stitch. Her knee was still throbbing from the fall in the stream. They both needed a rest, and there was no point in pretending they didn't.

'Take a rest,' she said.

'Can't risk it.'

'We've got to! We may have to keep going for hours. We've got to save some strength for later. Go on. Just a few minutes.'

'Well, maybe Ben could do with a rest,' he said.

They sat on separate tussocks of grass. Sam rubbed the backs of his legs. Gwynedd tried to wring some of the water from her sodden sleeves. She felt there was an immense distance between them.

'Bet you wish you were still in Bristol.'

'No,' he said. 'I just wish I was anywhere but here.'

She couldn't see, but she hoped he was smiling. The Halloween visit to the cottage had landed them in such a mess that they'd be lucky to get out of it alive. But they had rescued Ben. And if Sam was capable of making a joke, out here on this miserable hillside... Gwynedd felt a sudden surge of energy, determination, relief and hope. It was true. They had set out hours ago... no, they had set out *yesterday*... to save Ben, and they had done it. That was what mattered. All they had to do now was find a way of escaping the clutches of the Mangles and the jaws of their terrifying hound, and all would be well.

'Time to move.' She stood up.

'You don't think we could just lie here in the cold and wet for a few more hours? Pneumonia's beginning to seem like a good option.'

'You got to trust me, Sam.'

'I trust you. Though trusting you hasn't worked too well so far tonight.'

'Don't be so bloody ungrateful. *You* got us into this

mess. You and your bloody dog. *I'm* getting you out of it.'

'Sorry, Gwynedd. You lead, I'll follow.'

She couldn't recall any other time in her life when anyone had said "sorry" to her, and she had no idea what to say in reply, how to respond. She stumbled on, willing herself not to look back. Ben bounded past her. Good - if Ben was running on, Sam couldn't be far behind. He was coming. He was following her.

The wind grew stronger, and colder. It drove the chill through their wet clothing, on to their skin and into their flesh. And it bore with it ominous sounds... a rasping voice, more like beast than man, and a responding savage snarl, more like devil than dog.

'They're getting nearer.'

'Still got the stream to cross. That'll slow them down,' said Sam. 'Just keep going.'

They were both too tired to run, too tired to jog. She fancied she could have made slightly better speed on her own, but could no more think of leaving him than of surrendering. He was convinced that she was the one holding them back, but was determined to stick with her. Neither told the other what they were thinking. It was now simply a matter of walking, of dragging their bodies on and on.

They covered another couple of hundred metres of the sodden plateau before she looked back. She couldn't be sure – maybe it was imagination, maybe fear – but she thought she saw a figure on the skyline.

Len? She looked again, but the figure had disappeared.

'What is it?'

'Nothing,' she said.

They came at last to the stretch of Bryn Copra where the plateau ended and the land fell steeply, down to a track that wound its way through a narrow valley. Here they could move faster. Gwynedd plunged ahead.

'That's it!' she said. 'That's the drover's track to Llangurig...I'm sure it is.' Then she stopped.

Something was wrong. Down by the drover's track, there were two little circles, the moonlight reflected in something...

... something that could be the headlamps of a car... or an SUV.

They both dropped to the ground. Gwynedd raised her head, slowly. There was Mags, leaning on the bonnet, scanning the ridge through binoculars. She had chosen her spot well, for she could see up and down the narrow valley, and straight across it to the ridge of hills over which she had guessed the fugitives were most likely to appear. But, by the way she was moving the binoculars to and fro, she hadn't seen them yet.

'Stay down. Maybe we can crawl to that rock.'

They never had the chance to try. Gwynedd had forgotten their fellow fugitive. Ben had not stopped or dropped to the ground. He was trotting down the slope, heading for the track.

The binoculars came to rest for a split second, and then followed the dog's progress. Ben reached the drovers track at the bottom of the slope. Then he spun round, suddenly aware that he was on his own. He started back up the slope. The binoculars followed him.

'He's leading her straight to us.'

'He doesn't know that,' snapped Sam, but he wished Ben's love was matched with a little more intelligence. He called softly to the dog. Ben clattered over the rock to join them. 'Sit, Ben! Sit!' Ben danced about delightedly, thumping his tail and thrusting his wet nose into Sam's hand. Mags was now staring at their hiding place.

From the wastes of the plateau behind them came another burst of barking and snarling. Ben stopped dancing.

'If we can just get across the track...' said Gwynedd.

'What do we do then?'

'She can't follow us up that.' Gwynedd pointed across the valley, to the opposite slope. It was higher, steeper, and more formidable – a difficult place for sheep, an impossible route for any vehicle, even an SUV. 'Think we can make it?'

He gave her frozen hand a squeeze. 'Course we can... Ready? Let's go!'

They leapt up and went full pelt down the slope. As they ran, she saw Mags scramble into the SUV, start up, and swing the wheels to the right, aiming to cut off their line of flight.

Sam was ahead. 'Keep going!' he screamed over his shoulder.

Gwynedd's mind and heart were turning somersaults. Mags had a gun. She'd use it. She wouldn't. She would. She's mad. We'll make it. We won't. She'll run us down. She'll hit us before we can reach the track. We'll beat her to it. She'll hit Sam. She'll run him down. She'll kill us both...

Ben flashed across the track, well ahead of the SUV. Sam flung himself across, with seconds to spare, jumped up again as though he had bounced, and spun round. It was Gwynedd's turn... She had five metres to go... three... too late, too late! Sam saw her stumble, her body tipping further and further forward, the ground coming up to meet her. Mags slammed on the brake and stalled the engine. The SUV skidded over the grass and crunched to a halt. Gwynedd fell, but twisted sideways as she did so, and then rolled across the track almost under the vehicle's front wheels. Somebody screamed. Gwynedd reckoned it must have been her.

It was a Welsh bloody miracle. Gwynedd scrambled to her feet and raced on to join Sam.

Her body was weighed down with the wet of her garments. Her leg muscles were aching. Her arms were aching. Her hands were torn with cold. Her lungs were bursting within her chest. But they had to go on and on and on. Never mind the steep climb ahead. Think what's behind. Think of the gun, and climb, climb, climb! Never mind the SUV. Mags can't drive up here...

She began to count each jarring, bruising step....

216

Twelve... thirteen... fourteen, fifteen... then more slowly, up to twenty... twenty-one... up the hill. And she knew it would have to be another twenty, and another... and another. She was amazed to find that she could squeeze more effort from her poor, spent body, and risked raising her head to look ahead and see how Sam was doing. He was still going strong, hauling himself up the face of the hill. Good, good. Her eyes dully noted that there were slithers of track here, running along the contours of the mountain, tracks that could only have been made by sheep. Well, sheep were timid enough creatures, but they knew better than any human where it was safe to plant your feet. She could hear them sniffing, stirring in the nooks and crannies of the hillside, in which they nestled over-night, disturbed by these gasping, shaking, scurrying bodies, and frightened by the racing Ben.

A little below the crest of the steep hill, Sam reckoned it was safe enough to risk pausing for breath. Gwynedd struggled up to join him. She hugged him, and a sob broke from her.

'We made it!'

He hugged her. They collapsed into each other's arms, almost falling to the ground. She felt pain throughout her entire body. Her feet were sore and blistered. Her legs buckled with fatigue. The top half of her body was a mass of bruises. She looked back across the valley. Wonder of wonders! There was no sign of Mags and the SUV. Or of Len. And no sound of Beauty. The hunters must have given up the chase. For the moment, they were safe.

She was just beginning to believe that their luck might have changed, when the wind freshened, thick clouds rolled up, and it started to rain.

CHAPTER 19

They did their feeble best to shelter from the rain under a clump of threadbare rowan bushes. Images of warmth and safety floated through Gwynedd's brain. They were painful images. There were those relating to food, of all the meals she had cooked for Dave, of the few meals that other people had cooked for her, of the finest that chippies could offer. In her mind she saw massive fry-ups; sausages bursting from their skins on beds of creamy mashed potato; casseroles so tasty that you could see their flavour in the steam that rose from them; and Saqui's hot, crunchy, crispy chips. These agonising visions slipped away, and her mind went blank, only to rally and tease her with pictures of warm, thick blankets and soft, friendly pillows. Then the blankets disappeared, and she saw instead the fireplace in the front room of the bungalow. There were bright flames, and she could hear logs hissing and shifting and settling in the grate as the flames consumed them. Once or twice, her brain thrilled her with delightful fantasies of the Mangles driving the

SUV over a precipice, or coming to a cold and grisly end as it slipped into a reservoir full of the Welsh water that had plagued her and Sam for the past two miserable hours, in bog and stream and now rain.

The dream broke up, shattered by the intrusion of harsh, hungry, raw reality. She had little idea of where they were, but doubted that they were any nearer Llangurig than they had been when they first fled from the old mine. There were still miles to go before they could find help.

It seemed to Gwynedd that they had only two choices. They could press on for Llangurig, which would certainly mean more climbing, crossing more streams, floundering through more bogs; and would probably mean getting lost. If that happened they would die of exposure. Funny – she had always thought that people only died of exposure on foreign mountains, where everything was always ice and snow. Now she realised that her own Welsh mountains were cruel enough to kill.

What else could they do? Well, they could risk heading back to rejoin the drover's road to Rhayader, but hoping to strike it somewhere above the little bridge, a mile or two nearer home. In that vague direction there were one or two lonely farms set back from the road, the nearest five miles or more away. They could head for that. Maybe there'd be a proper miracle – not like the half-hearted disappointment they'd already suffered - and a truck or car would come along and give them a lift back to town, back to Dave's bungalow. At the thought of her own bed she could feel tears bubbling up. More bloody water. She pushed the thought away. They weren't real tears, she told herself. They were just drops of tiredness.

'Where do we go?' said Sam.

'Down towards the road.'

It was a risk, however. If the Mangles hadn't given up the hunt, they could well be waiting down on the road.

'They know where I live, and they must have guessed that you're staying with me. They'll expect us to be heading back that way. There's dozens of places along that road where they could ambush us...' She fell silent. The comforting picture of the Mangles driving into a reservoir had turned into a nightmare image of two teenagers with their heads bashed in, sinking to the bottom of a long-drowned valley. Best not to share that with Sam. It didn't matter how good a swimmer you were – on a night like this no one would last more than a couple of minutes in water as cold and as deep as that.

It was up to her to make the decision. 'We'll head for home.'

'You don't sound very sure,' said Sam.

'What am I supposed to do? I ain't got a crystal ball. I ain't even got a bloody map, which wouldn't be any bloody good anyway, since your bloody torch don't work no more.'

They walked on in silence.

The rain trickled down – softer now, but cold and

clinging. They followed the track back to the road, reaching it much closer to the mine than either they had hoped or wanted. They trudged on, towards the bridge, barely aware of their surroundings. To their right was the Afon Ystwyth, at its wildest and widest, already gurgling and foaming with rain water draining from the mountain-sides. To their left was a small grove of trees. Here, a flock of sheep had clustered together, coughing like humans, but catching the warmth of each other's bodies while the rain trickled from their wool. Sam called Ben to his side. He didn't want the dog to stray and frighten the sheep.

Even on the road, their pace was still agonisingly slow. They approached the bridge. The road curved here, and a stone wall hid all but the crest of the bridge from their view. They rounded the bend, with some fifty metres still to go before they would reach the bridge. And suddenly, light blazed out, blinding them. They stared stupidly ahead, shielding their eyes from the light, guessing that it came from the headlights of a vehicle, and needing no second guess as to whose vehicle it was.

A voice ordered them to stay where they were. It was an unnecessary command, for they were both incapable of movement. For what seemed a long time there was no sound save the rushing of the river and the unsettled snuffling of the sheep. Then they heard the voice again, from behind the light, not as loud this time, but more sinister.

'All right, Len. We've got them. Now... what the hell

do we do with them?'

'We don't do anything. Beauty'll see to them.'

'No, Len.'

'Every dog must have his day, Mags, and this is Beauty's day.'

It was the end. Both Gwynedd and Sam knew that. Even if they had had any strength left, there was no way for them to turn. The road, the river, the little grove of trees... this was their entire world. This was all they had. This was where it would end.

'Let's get the business done and get the hell out.' Len bent down to unfasten Beauty's chain.

'God Almighty! You can't let the dog do it!'

The dog was already over-excited. Len's fingers were cold, and he was having difficulty unfastening the chain round Beauty's neck. He swore as he worked at the clip, and muttered to himself.

'All me and Beauty are after is satisfaction... Stand still!... And a clear conscience. You can't shoot kids and get away with it... What's the matter with this bloody clip... Still, damn you!... That's why we're not having any shooting, Mags...'

Mags pulled at his arm. 'Please, Len. Let the kids go!'

'You read about it all the time in the papers. Kid killed by savage dog... Do you hear me?... Don't you bloody *move*!...'

There was no way of telling from his snarling voice if the man was talking to his dog or his wife. All three were losing control.

'But with Beauty here... Still, I said!!!!...'

The more he swore, the more he tugged at the chain, the more both Mangles screamed and shouted at each other, the wilder the dog became. The shivering children could still see little of what was happening, but they heard the rattle of the dog's chain and the snarling of the dog. They also heard, dimly, the uneasy snuffling and bleating of nearby sheep. The sheep had sensed the presence of dog for some time. Now, the roaring and shouting and Beauty's growling made them take fright. They started moving in clumsy panic along the wire fence that separated their field from the road.

Sam felt Gwynedd's cold hand reach into his. He grasped it tightly.

At last Len had managed to release the catch. 'Go get 'em, Beauty!'

There was a cry of horror from Mags. The light snapped off, and Sam and Gwynedd were blinded anew by the darkness.

It was their own complete exhaustion that saved them. They could not move. Escape was impossible. All they could do was scream, and they did that... loudly. The sound was enough to drive the sheep over the edge of fear into blind panic. The creatures butted into each other, turning this way and that, unable to find a way out of danger. Bleating pitifully, the compact mass of wool began to unravel at the edges, the leaders and flankers breaking into a run that prompted the whole flock to stampede.

Too late, Len realised that this fearful diversion was an irresistible lure to Beauty. He had already unfastened the dog's chain, and the beast had charged – not at Gwynedd and Sam – but at the sheep. The remnants of the flock broke and scattered. Beauty swerved from the road and set off in pursuit. Len hurled himself after the dog, cursing and swearing, and lashing out with the chain in a vicious attempt to beat the dog into control. But the dog was too fast for him, and it rushed on.

There was a wild bleating of terror from the sheep as the dog ran among them. Against the dark hillside it was just possible to make out stragglers from the flock stumble and fall, as though pulled down by the dog. Sam and Gwynedd could guess what was happening, and they could hear Len bellowing and raging at his precious animal.

'For the love of Jesus, Mags! Up here! And bring the gun!'

Gwynedd waited until she was sure that Mags had set off after Len before letting go of Sam's hand.

For a moment she dared not speak, believing that somehow, amid all the chaos and confusion on the hillside, Len or Mags would hear her voice, and hurry back to settle matters. Eventually she plucked up the courage to whisper to Sam: 'Where's Ben?'

They found Ben a little way off, backed up against a dry stone wall. The dog was trembling, but safe. Sam's hand was still shaking as he stroked it.

'What do we do now?'

'Let's have a look in their posh car.'

They peered in through the windows, just in case there were more dogs hidden inside. Then they opened the doors.

'Can you drive?'

'Yeah,' she said. 'And fly. Don't be daft. When do I ever get the chance to sit in a car, let alone learn to drive it? Tell you what, though… let's just see what the Mangles have left us.'

They went through the dashboard and the pockets in the doors. They found some sweets, and two packets of cigarettes.

'No matches,' said Gwynedd. 'That's a shame.'

'Did you want a smoke?'

'No, silly. I thought we might torch their car. That'd stop them chasing us, and give you a chance to dry your poor trainers.'

'It would bring them back,' he said. 'When the tank exploded.'

He was right. Safety before revenge, that was the first law of survival. She thought of releasing the handbrake and letting the car roll off the road until it crunched into the stone wall. But the slope was too gentle, and neither of them had the energy to push.

She helped herself to a rug and a golfing umbrella, as well as the sweets. 'Come on, last leg.'

At first, Gwynedd brandished the Mangles' umbrella proudly above them, while Sam held the rug tight against his body. But the brolly was heavy, and her arms began to ache. They limped a mile along the deserted road. They knew there was no way they could reach Rhayader, and there was no sign of a farmhouse. It was Sam who spotted the primitive remains of a shepherd's hut, a few metres above the road. There was little enough of it left, but it offered some slight shelter from the wind and the rain. They stumbled to it, kicked a few stones aside to create a place that they could lie on, and settled down.

'Our first night truly together,' she said.

They shared the last of the sweets. 'Your Becky wouldn't like you sleeping with a girl, not without having brushed your teeth.'

'Oh, do shut up.'

They tried to keep watch, peering down at the road, listening fearfully for any sound of the Mangles' return, but their eyes refused to stay open. They curled up together, sharing the rug, and it wasn't long before they fell asleep, with Ben's twitching body sprawled on top of them. Gwynedd's last thought was to wonder if the dog would generate enough heat to keep them alive till morning.

They never heard the sounds of a shotgun being discharged across the valley.

CHAPTER 20

Two sausages, two rashers, two eggs, mushrooms and tomatoes, and not a trace of fat. Gwynedd gazed at the plate the woman had placed in front of her, savouring that last moment of ravenous hunger before starting on a pile of food. It had been a long time since someone had cooked her breakfast. There used to be bowls of cold stodgy cereal in the old days, and jam sandwiches that ma made, but she'd never had anything half as succulent and delicious as this.

The woman adjusted the blanket round Sam's shoulders, and sat down to join them at the table. 'Out on the hills all night... you could have died.'

'We nearly did,' said Sam.

As she crammed the good food into her mouth, Gwynedd prepared for the many problems ahead. They'd rescued Ben. They'd got away from the Mangles. Now came a much harder task – keeping Sam's gob shut. They'd had no time to plan and agree a story, a done and dusted explanation as to why they'd been out on the mountains all night. The first thing to do was to keep Sam's mouth filled with food so he wouldn't talk. Becky must have taught him not to speak with his gob full.

'Don't let all this lovely food go cold,' she said, and fetched Sam a kick under the table.

They had been found shortly after dawn. A sheep farmer patrolling his hills had stumbled upon them, shaken them from their sleep, and brought them back to the low-ceilinged kitchen of the farmhouse. By nature, he was a man who spoke little, and he had asked them no questions. Immediately they had reached the farm, he had called his wife. She had stripped them of their sopping clothes, swathed them in towels and blankets, and brought them to sit at the long wooden table in the warmth of the kitchen. Gwynedd had relished every moment. Sam had tried to hide his embarrassment. He had made a feeble protest when Ben had not been allowed in the kitchen.

On the few occasions when the farmer did speak, his words had authority. 'Houses are for people. Yards are for dogs,' he said.

Gwynedd ate. Her body was making a rapid recovery. Now her mind got going. Not many people would believe what had happened. The only person who'd swallow a tale like that would be Little Huwie. Becky might, but if she did, she'd also do her nut and not let Sam out of her sight for the next fifty years. Dave might, but he and Horseface would turn it all round and use it as evidence that she should be banged up in a kids' home straightaway. The only person who'd believe every word of it would be Mollie, because by now she probably knew it was true.

The Mangles would say Gwynedd was a liar, and cite the visits to the camp as proof that she was a nosey trouble-maker, with some stupid grudge against them. Len and Mags were slippery customers who'd say it was all some wicked story that she and Sam had cooked up. The police would take the Mangles' side. Where was there any proof of what really happened? Tyre marks on the old drovers' road? That would prove nothing. A couple of spent cartridge cases up at the mill? If Len hadn't removed them already, he'd say they came from target practice or shooting at vermin. The Mangles would be able to walk away, free and apparently innocent. They'd go on living at the cottage, ten minutes walk from the bungalow, real cosy and neighbourly. There was no one Gwynedd could trust on this one, and she was getting no help from her inner voice, which had said nothing for over twelve hours now. She reckoned it had died.

'What was it?' said the woman. 'Some kind of survival test?'

Gwynedd nodded. Maybe it would be best to say as little as possible, whether it was the truth or lies.

The woman looked doubtful. 'You're too young for that. And whoever organised it should have more sense than to send you out with just one blanket and an umbrella between you.'

Gwynedd knew that Sam was watching her closely. Still she could think of nothing to say.

'Teachers was it? You'd think teachers would have more sense. What school are you from?'

'Sebastien Cabot,' said Sam.

'I've not heard of that one,' said the woman. 'Where is it?'

It was time to take control and change the subject - fast. 'Could I have some more toast, please,' said Gwynedd. 'But everything's fine now, Sam. Isn't it! All over and done with.' She couldn't trust him to speak. Sam had no idea how and when a full and frank confession and a tissue of lies could overlap.

The woman brought the toast to the table, and stood over them like a mother hen. 'Now,' she said, 'once you've eaten, the first thing is to get you phoning your parents to let them know you're all right. The phone's by the front door.'

'We can't,' said Sam. 'Our mum's at work.'

'Your mum?' The woman looked from Gwynedd to Sam, and back again. 'You're not brother and sister! Can't be... not when one of you's bl...' She was embarrassed, and checked herself. 'Well, what about your school? They'll need to know where you are. What time were they supposed to collect you?'

'We're supposed to find out own way back,' said Sam.

'Where to?'

'Rhayader.'

The woman was appalled at the lack of care given to these children. 'That's absurd! They leave you out on the hillside all night, with nothing to eat...'

'We did have food,' said Sam. 'They gave us plenty of

232

food, but we ate it all last night.' He recalled a phrase of that Becky used frequently. 'You know how badly organised kids are.'

'What about your dad... your dads?'

This was an easy question, one Sam could answer truthfully. 'My dad's dead, and we don't know where Gwynedd's dad is.'

The woman frowned. 'I don't know what to make of the pair of you.'

'It's no good, Sam,' said Gwynedd. 'We'll have to do as this lady says, and tell her the truth. It's like this – we were out with a group of friends – you know, having a bit of Halloween fun – but me and this other girl had a row, and because of that the group split up. So, next thing is, Sam and me got lost. Ma won't be worried because she thinks we're stopping over with friends in town. She'll only worry if she finds out... well, if she finds out about the row. And we don't want to worry her, do we?'

'And what happened?' said the woman.

'It was Ben's fault...our dog. He run off and we couldn't catch him. And then Sam fell over...show your bruises, Sam. And look at my knee! And it came on to rain and we were too tired to go back.'

'Are you trying to tell me you chased your dog all the way here from Rhayader? Twelve miles or more!' The woman looked from one to the other. 'I don't believe you,' she said.

Gwynedd spoke quickly. 'Well, the truth is we did it for a dare. The girl we were stopping over with, she dared us to stay out all night. And we thought we'd go for a walk up in the mountains, 'cos Sam loves the mountains, don't you, Sam... yes, you do... you know you do... and since he's moved to Bristol he hasn't seen much of the mountains, and being half-term we didn't have to go to school today and I guess we must have just not realised how far we were walking and then it rained, and that was awful...'

'I don't believe you,' the woman repeated.

Sam roused himself. 'It started with Ben,' he said.

'The dog?'

'My dog. There were these people...'

'Don't tell her!'

Sam shook his head, but he never got a chance to begin his tale, for the kitchen door was flung open and the sheep farmer strode into the room. He was thunderously angry. He dragged a chair across to the table and dropped heavily into it, facing the children.

'And what the hell did you think you were playing at, on my hills last night?' He slammed his hand on the table. 'It'll cost your parents a pretty penny when all this is sorted out. And you can say goodbye to that dog of yours. I'll shoot him myself if I have to...'

The woman got up and stood behind him, her hands on his shoulders. 'Trouble?' she said, gently.

'Three ewes killed. Six or seven maimed. Dozens more driven crazy with fright.' He shook off the woman's hands, and started pacing about the kitchen. 'Ain't you got no more sense than take a brute dog out on the hills where there's sheep? God above, don't you know the damage you done?'

'It wasn't us…' Sam wanted to explain. This was dreadful. They'd rescued Ben from one madman and now another wanted to kill him. 'It wasn't us. It was…'

Gwynedd's foot only just reached Sam's shins, but it stopped him saying more.

'So, who was it? Are you telling me there was others up to no good on my hills in the night? The whole place crawling with kids and dogs they couldn't control, was it? Well, there's one way to sort this. Let's have the police up here.' He snatched the phone from its cradle on the window-sill.

They waited for the arrival of the police. Sam listened to the ticking of the kitchen clock and darted terrified glances at the man who was threatening to shoot Ben. Gwynedd didn't hear the clock. She was still trying to construct a watertight explanation of their soggy adventures, one that would satisfy Becky and Dave, the farmer and the woman, social services, the police, and her own hunger for a bit of self-respect. The woman tried to get her to talk, warning her that the truth would come out in the end.

But there had to be a better solution than the truth. Gwynedd thought hard about what she wanted. Ben to live, Sam to be happy, Becky and Dave not to moan, Horseface to back off, and someone – anyone – to recognise that what she and Sam had done was brave and good. They'd never quitted, not even with a loaded gun pointing at them. That should make people sit up.

She'd like her ma and dad to get to hear of that.

'Life must go on,' said the woman, and went out to feed the hens.

It was worse in the kitchen once she had gone. The farmer drank his tea and sat in silence. Gwynedd looked at him - a big, powerful man with his mind made up. The Mangles would get off free, because they were dangerous and cunning and frightening. Guilty or innocent, Ben would be shot because he was weak and unwanted. Gwynedd knew she'd be in trouble because no one cared enough about her. If only one person… that was all it took, one person, to turn misery into happiness, death into life.

The kitchen clock went on ticking.

Eventually, a police car drew up. The woman returned to the kitchen, followed by a cop who exchanged friendly greetings with the farmer.

'So – what have we got here?' said the cop.

The farmer explained how he had found the children and their dog, then about the dead sheep on the hillside 'You'll have that dog put down,' he demanded, 'or I'll do it myself.'

The cop smiled grimly. 'Anything to oblige,' he said, 'but I don't reckon that's necessary. We've already come across a dead hound out on the road by the old mines. It's been shot. And, from the blood on its mouth and the wisps of wool in its teeth, I'd say there was enough evidence to suggest that it was the beast that had a go at your sheep. Took some lifting, but I've got the corpse in the boot of the car. Don't suppose you killed that one?'

The farmer shook his head.

'Didn't think so. Whoever did may have been more interested in protecting themselves than any sheep. There's a trace of denim in the dog's mouth. We'll have to get a whole lot of tests done. Its owner could have found it impossible to quieten the dog down once it had got a taste for blood, like, so the dog turned on the owner. Trouble is, it's highly unlikely we'll ever discover who that was...'

'We know who it was,' said Sam.

'And who are you?' said the cop.

'I'm Sam Harper.'

For a second, Gwynedd considered giving her usual false name – Marilyn Jones. But the truth came blurting out. 'I'm Gwynedd Hughes,' she said.

'Just a minute...' The cop flicked through the pages of his notebook. 'Don't anyone up here ever listen to our excellent local radio station?' he said.

'Got better things to do,' mumbled the farmer. 'Trying to keep my bloody sheep alive.'

'Here we are... "Gwynedd Hughes and Sam Harper" ...that right? "Missing all night". He turned to Gwynedd. 'Now, young lady, your Grandad down in Rhayader been doing his pieces over what might have happened to the pair of you. That's why I was out on the road so early, looking for you. OK, first thing is to let everyone know you're safe, and where you are. Have to do that from the car.' He fingered the radio on his lapel. 'This thing don't work half the time in these hills.'

He went out.

The woman smiled and said: 'So it weren't your dog did the damage. I'm glad.'

The farmer looked at Sam and Gwynedd. 'I'll want proof it wasn't your dog,' he said.

The room fell silent again until the cop returned. 'Now, then,' he said. 'What you two been up to?'

Sam looked at Gwynedd. She smiled at him, took a deep breath and launched into an account of what had happened. It was lengthy and richly coloured, and Sam hardly recognised himself as the brave hero of the night's events, but it was essentially the truth. At the end of it, the cop asked Sam if he had anything to add.

'It was my fault,' he said. 'It's my dog. And it was Gwynedd who saved him...saved all of us.'

The farmer still wanted justice. 'And you'd both stand up in court and repeat all this? That bloke won't walk free. Not if I have my way.'

'How about it?' said the cop. He looked first at Sam, who said nothing. The cop raised his eyebrows and turned to Gwynedd.

'What would happen to the Mangles?' she said. 'If they went to court? If they were found guilty?'

'Hard to tell,' said the cop. 'That's not up to us. They'd have to pay compensation for the sheep. If the court believed your story the bloke might go to prison for a few months. The woman...? Maybe a month, maybe a suspended sentence. Longer if you could convince the court how she'd threatened you. But that would be difficult, you being... well, youngsters.'

'Yeah,' said Gwynedd. Funny how old people – like judges and teachers and social workers – didn't trust young people's memories. 'So, that's it then. The Mangles come back and go on living in the cottage, down the lane from me and Dave. And I pass the place every day on the way to school, because they'll be out before I've left school. And every morning we say "nice day" to each other, is that it? Even if they go to prison, they come back and I have to go on living with them as neighbours.'

The cop nodded.

'But you can't,' said Sam.

'So long as Ben's safe, I can keep out of their way. All this was for Ben, wasn't it? Well, if they've not got him, that's OK. They've got no hold over me, but I've got a hold over them. They wouldn't dare touch me with what I know about them. But once I tell what I know, and they've been punished... then I got no hold over them. Don't you see?' She'd thought about this, and about what would happen to Mollie if the Mangles went to prison. She'd be put in a home, and Gwynedd didn't wish that on anyone, not even that cow. And suppose it was the same home that Horseface and Dave had lined up for her...

Sam shook his head, but as she drew her foot back to kick him, he reached across the table and took hold of her hand.

'What about my sheep? Three ewes dead. Three more I can't save, that's for certain... what about that?' The farmer looked at Gwynedd and Sam as though he still held them responsible.

'If we can match the blood on the dead hound's mouth with the blood of your sheep, you can get the owner for damage in a civil court, with an order to have the hound destroyed. That'd be overdoing it a bit, the hound being already dead.' The cop hoped to see a few smiles, but the faces round the room remained grim. The cop plunged on. 'But these other matters... that's criminal business. That's up to this young lady and gentleman. Without their evidence, there's no case against Mr and Mrs... er, Mangles. Funny thing, that's not a name I recognise from round these parts...Tell you who they do remind me of, though. That couple out in the woods on the Cwmcoch road. Mr and Mrs Franklin, isn't it? Very like them, these Mangles sound. And it does remind me...we ought to be paying Mr and Mrs Franklin a visit. I know the health inspectors were worried some time back about the condition of that camp. RSPCA might be concerned, too. And the dog-fights will certainly interest them. We'll book a little time to get together and all go out there for a chat.'

So that was how it worked. It was a carve-up, a deal, just like what went on at school. "I'll trade my skateboard for your flash trainers." "You give us that Quiksilver sweatshirt and you can have my new Reeboks." "You clear up your camp in the woods and we'll say nothing about what happened at the mine." Adults were just like kids, only more powerful.

A car drew up outside. This would be Becky and

Dave arriving. Gwynedd braced herself. She could deal with cops and angry farmers, and even with Len - so long as he didn't have a gun in his hands - but Dave was different. He'd got what he wanted, served up on a plate - an excuse to get rid of her. He'd have her out of the bungalow and in a kids' home before nightfall. Well, she wouldn't go down without a fight.

The cop looked out of the window. 'Didn't take them long,' he said.

Becky was first into the kitchen, closely followed by Dave. The old man grabbed Gwynedd and yanked her from her chair. He shook her fiercely before wrapping her in his arms and holding her tight.

'You stupid, stupid girl,' he gasped. 'Don't you know better than to give me a scare like that? And me, near out of my mind with worry for you.'

He stank of cigarettes. He hadn't shaved. His face was rough with bristles, sharp with cold. He was shaking. At first she assumed it was with anger, but then she heard him give what sounded like a sob. She wanted to look at his face, to see if there were tears in his eyes, but he held her so tight she couldn't break away. Over Dave's shoulder, she could see Becky hugging Sam, but Becky was smiling with relief. Gwynedd watched, as Becky gave Sam a gentle kiss, and then held him at arm's length, as though for inspection. That must be how people behaved when they loved each other.

Then Dave let go. She peered at him. There *were* tears in his eyes, but she didn't get no gentle kiss. Some hopes, she thought. Instead, he went on the attack.

'I know what you bin doing,' he said. 'I can guess where you went last night. Word gets around. There was dogs matched against each other, out at the old mines, and you was there... don't try to deny it. I told you to keep your nose out, Gwynedd love, but you *never* listen!'

It was the first time he'd called her 'Gwynedd love' in years. But she was confused: one moment he was hugging her, the next he was having a go at her.

Then he said: 'Oh, Gwynedd, I bin worried sick for you.'

She was stunned. What did it mean? Maybe he didn't want to put her in a home after all. Maybe he wanted her to stay in the bungalow, and not just to get his meals, do the shopping and keep the place tidy. Maybe he loved her. What did that mean? Was he going to make her cry? She looked across to Sam and Becky for guidance.

Becky was still holding Sam. 'You're safe,' she said.

'Yeah,' said Sam. 'Ben's safe, too.'

Sam and Becky sat down together. Dave joined them at the table, and patted the bench beside him. He looked up at Gwynedd. 'Come and sit here beside me,' he said. 'And let's have the whole story... the truth, mind.'

She did as she was told, and he put out a bony hand to take hold of hers. It was like the action of a child. Perhaps things would change, maybe they already had. She wondered if she would have to be the adult now. The day might not be far off when, if she called Sam "her darling", or held his hand, or invited him to stay, it would carry deeper meaning.

Gwynedd made up her mind. She would tell no lies, but not everything had changed. She would still hold back some of the truth. The adults wouldn't be able to take it all. As the story of last night's events unfolded, all went well, until Sam mentioned the gun. The colour drained from Becky's face, and she ordered the cop to arrest the Mangles immediately. Still trying to protect Mollie, Gwynedd said there was no need for that, but Becky paid no attention. Fortunately, she attached more attention to what the cop and the woman had to say. Gwynedd could see that the cop had convinced himself that her report of the night's activities was richly coloured.

'It may not be as bad as it seems, Mrs Harper,' he said. 'There was a gun out on these hills last night, but the only victim was a dog, and that dog had it coming, anyhow. This young couple may well have had a bit of a fright, but they're none the worse for wear. And they've worked up quite a tale to tell their mates.' He winked at Gwynedd, as though he knew what she was up to. 'We may well be contacting your son and this young lady to clear up one or two points. Otherwise, I don't think there's anything to worry about.' He left.

It seemed to Gwynedd that the cop had spoken to everyone as though they were all kids: "there, there, it's all right" when it bloody wasn't. He was trying to make everything sound cosy and nice for Becky and Dave, because they'd sleep better if they believed the

Mangles had had their teeth drawn. Keep the adults happy and it's up to them to keep the kids happy. Well, that might work with some families, but it had never worked with her and Dave, and it could never have worked with ma and dad – else they'd be here, now.

The farmer stood up, apologised for losing his temper, and repeated several times that he was glad it wasn't their dog that had gone for his sheep. He spoke only a few words to Gwynedd and Sam. 'Got nothing against dogs,' he assured them. 'In their place.' Then he left.

Gwynedd watched the woman make yet more toast and pots of tea, and listened with one ear to what Becky was saying to Sam, and with half an ear to what Dave was saying to everyone in the kitchen. She heard Becky explain how she'd become worried when Sam hadn't phoned to say he was safely installed in Gwynedd's bungalow, had tried phoning him and had got no answer.

'So I guessed you'd gone out Halloweening and were having such a good time you'd forgotten about phoning. So I phoned your mobile again, late...'

Gwynedd thought of the moment when Sam's mobile had dropped over the edge of the roof out at the mine, and how she had feared that he'd go with it. She wondered if that was when Becky was trying to call him.

'... and in the end I phoned Mrs Rhys, our old neighbour, and asked her to pop up to the bungalow to check all was well. Which it wasn't.' Becky was still angry.

'And Mrs Rees give me this piece of paper with Becky's number on it, and I go tramping all the way to the phone box by the Triangle Inn, long after midnight, to tell Becky here that Gwynedd and Sam were missing and nobody had a clue where they might be.' Dave was angry, too.

Gwynedd could imagine Dave hobbling through the night without a clue as to who to contact. He'd gone to the phone box because he was frightened, needed help, needed to know who was going to make his tea in the morning. Still, phoning Bristol, even after midnight, must have cost him a pound or two.

'Fortunately, Martin was with me,' said Becky, 'and he was wonderful. He insisted on driving me here, and he phoned the police and gave them your mobile number, Sam, and we kept trying it, but it didn't seem to work…'

Gwynedd was interested in the mention of Martin. So, Becky's fancy man was right by Becky's side when Dave's call had come through… after midnight. Maybe there were other adventures last night.

'…it was three in the morning when we got to Rhayader.' Becky continued her story. 'We went straight to the bungalow and waited, and waited. Sam, I was so worried. Martin called the police again, to give them *his* mobile number, but it wasn't until about half an hour ago that they called back with the news.'

'Is that Martin out in the car?' Gwynedd had nipped across to the window that faced the farmhouse yard and peered at the silver saloon parked in the November sunshine. She might tell Dave what had happened to her mobile later... much later.

'The poor man must be wondering what's going on.' Becky smiled at the woman. 'Would it be all right if a friend of mine came in?'

Bloomin' heck! "A friend"! Gwynedd almost snorted.

Becky turned to Sam. She was blushing. 'There's something you should know,' she said. 'Martin's decided to move nearer work. He's bought a house, not far from us. With a big garden. How about Ben living there?'

This wasn't about Ben. No way.

CHAPTER 21

She was exhausted. Only the hunger of curiosity prevented her falling asleep in Martin's large and comfortable car as they drove back to the bungalow. The moment they arrived, Dave brought up the subject of his delayed breakfast.

'But you get to bed, Gwynedd girl. You been through a lot. There's no need for you to fuss over me. Do me good to fend for myself, once in a while. And I'll see to that daft dog you brought back with you. After all, you won't always be here to look after me.'

Just for a moment Gwynedd's fears came back. So he did want to get rid of her. Then she looked at him, and realised she'd got it all wrong... perhaps she'd been getting it wrong for years. Perhaps he'd never wanted to get rid of her. She was touched. So it was possible for some things to change, after all. She gave him a hug, and headed for her room and her bed. As she opened the door, she heard Dave giving Becky his breakfast order. When Gwynedd woke, three hours later, Sam was still asleep on the couch in the front room. She could hear Becky, Martin and Dave trying to make conversation in the tiny kitchen. She dressed and went to the front room.

She found Sam still asleep, with Ben in his arms.

'Wakey, wakey, Sam darling.'

He raised a head still heavy with sleep from the cushion. 'Any nightmares?' he said.

'Only one where you was chasing me, and no matter how slow I went you still couldn't catch me. Now, get up and get dressed.'

She would have liked to slip away from the adults, to take Sam into town, to revisit their old haunts, to eat doughnuts, to meet up with the gang, to find Mollie and check that she was OK. Last night had been a triumph, but not one she could celebrate until she knew Mollie was safe.

She didn't get what she wanted. Martin insisted on taking them all out for what he called "lunch" at the Castle Hotel. Ben was left on Martin's discarded copy of *The Times* to sleep off the effects of a night on the bare mountain. On the way into town, crammed together with Dave in the back of Martin's car, Sam whispered to Gwynedd that he'd much rather they were going to the chippie. She gave his hand a squeeze. She wanted to give him a kiss. The rest of the journey she stared at the back of Martin and Becky's heads.

They left the car in the car park and walked to the hotel, bumping into Vinnie and Little Huwie at the corner of North Street. It was an irresistible opportunity to show off. She linked arms with Martin, leaning intimately towards him. He made no attempt to pull away. 'Hi, Vinnie,' she said.

'Gwyn! You missed all the fun last night. We was all sick as dogs down the rec.'

'We're just off for *lunch* at the Castle,' said Gwynedd.

Little Huwie was shocked 'That's haunted,' he said. 'By the ghost of a woman that ate her husband there years ago, in a war, when there was what they called food rationing. Anyone stays the night there alone goes mad, bites bits out of people. Oh, hallo, Mrs Harper. Hallo, Sam. How you getting on? Bristol, isn't it? That's a dangerous place. They got all manner of drugs there. You best come back.'

'Anyone seen Mollie?' Gwynedd put the question as casually as she could.

'Not this morning,' said Vinnie. 'Still recovering from last night, I reckon.'

'What happened to her?'

Sam heard the anxiety in Gwynedd's voice.

'Drunk. Washed out,' said Vinnie. 'Stumbling and mumbling about the place. Fancies you, Sam, she does. Don't see it myself, but there we are.' He smiled up at Martin. 'You must be Gwyn's dad.'

Martin withdrew his arm. They moved on, Sam and Gwynedd bringing up the rear. At the hotel, Dave held the door open for them to enter. 'Go on, love,' he said to Gwynedd. 'All this is thanks to you.'

They sat in what Martin called the *lounge*, and had what he called *aperitifs*. Gwynedd had an ice-laden glass of coke, most of which she spilled on the floor.

Martin said it didn't matter, but Gwynedd could see that it did. There's liars everywhere, she thought.

She was rattled. The whole adventure should have had "happy ending" written all over it, but she didn't feel happy. Ben was safe. Sam was happy. Martin and Becky were happy. Dave seemed happy, eating everything that was put in front of him without a single complaint. Funny how he'd held the door open for her. And strange to hear him call her 'love'. Earlier, at the farm, he'd used her name... and those tears in his eyes. There was no way he was planning to have her taken into care. That was good, but there were still things to worry about. She heard Martin and Becky discussing a plan to take Sam back to Bristol tonight. She'd half expected this. But what really worried her was Mollie.

As soon as the meal was finished, she and Sam left the adults at the hotel and walked together out of town, to climb the hill behind the cottage. She gazed down at Sam's old home. There were no signs that anyone was in, but further away a wisp of smoke arose from the pine wood. The Mangles had returned to their lair.

'Rat kebab for Christmas dinner,' said Sam

She was puzzled. 'What you on about?'

'It's what you said, about the Mangles. That night when we came up here with Ben... the night I stayed at your bungalow. We saw smoke coming from their camp, and you said they were having rat kebab for their dinner.'

'For their *tea*,' she corrected him. She had forgotten, but was touched that he had remembered. She put her arm round him. He didn't move away.

'Will you be all right?' said Sam.

'Course I'll be all right,' she said. 'Len and Mags won't dare touch me. And Dave's learned his lesson. However much he moans, he can't live without me, so he won't have me put away. Horseface'll back off, because if she puts me in care, she'll have to find someone else to look after Dave. And that'll cost. That's how it works. That's money. That's the way of the world.'

'What about Ben coming to Bristol?'

'That lets us off the hook. You can give up your mad plan to make Ben a hideaway down by the river, and I don't have to waste my time feeding him twice a day and taking him for walks. It would never have worked, anyhow. Of *course* your stupid dog should move to Bristol. Then, when you come to Wales, you come to see me, not some rotten old dog.' She was being serious. Sam's laugh disappointed her.

They sat together on the hillside, with the town spread out below them.

'Do you still climb on the swings, and do your acrobatics, on the way to school?'

'No. Finished with all that ages ago.' She felt uncomfortable. That was in the days when she and Sam had a present as well as a past. Right now, what they needed was a future. 'There's holidays,' she said.

'Not till Christmas. And we always go to my nan's for Christmas.'

She knew that. Every Christmas the Harper cottage had been empty. Every Christmas, she and Dave sat opposite each other at the little table in the front room, eating their Christmas dinner. It was the one day in the year when they ate together, chewing their way through her brave attempts at a full roast, which had never come out right. The gravy was too thin, the bread sauce was too thick, the turkey was too dry, the sprouts were too wet, and she always left it too late to buy the only brand of packet stuffing that he liked. Every Christmas, she had left him to sleep through the Queen's Speech and a welter of movies on TV. Her own great escape was to find mates in town – some mates, Vinnie and Little Huwie! Nothing was open, no shops, no caffs, but they all wrapped up well against the cold and grumbled contentedly together, about the presents they had wanted and the presents they had got. Last year there was Mollie, and all her presents were bloody marvellous, apparently, which provoked an extra bad row, instead of a Christmas truce. Gwynedd had never told Sam, but Christmas was the time she missed him most.

'I'll have to see what Vinnie's up to this Christmas.' It was a tease without sparkle. She didn't dare to suggest that she might come to Bristol after Christmas. The bungalow would then be full of food: cold turkey, left-over Christmas pudding, mince pies, beer, and stacks of ciggie tobacco. Dave could manage on his own with all that. She could save up for her fare and get away for two or three days. It would be wonderful.

She was about to grab him, put her arms round him, hold him tight, when she saw someone climbing the hill and heading towards them.

'It's Mollie,' said Sam.

They sat in silence until Mollie reached them. She was out of breath. She looked ill. Last night had taken its effect.

'I saw you from the cottage,' said Mollie. 'From your old bedroom, Sam. I just wanted to say... to tell you... to ask...'

'Is it about last night?' said Sam.

'Course it's about bloody last night! You're mad, both of you. You could have been killed.'

'We nearly were,' said Gwynedd. 'Your mum and dad both wanted to do away with us.'

'Why did you do it?' said Mollie.

'To save Ben's life,' said Sam.

'You risked your lives for the sake of that weedy little runt! Makes no sense.' Mollie looked at Gwynedd. 'That ain't why *you* did it, was it? You did it for him.' She jerked her head in Sam's direction, and then blinked with pain. Last night's drinking had left her with a bad headache. 'Mad. What good would it have done either of you if you'd been killed?'

They didn't respond. The sun had set behind the mountains, and it was getting cold. Gwynedd shivered.

'We ought to go,' said Sam.

'Lucky bastards,' said Mollie. 'That's what you two are... lucky bastards. You've got each other. I wouldn't have risked my life to bring that dog back to you, Sam Harper. No one would. Except her. And now she's got you. Stupid, lucky bastards.' She started back down the hillside.

Gwynedd called after her. 'Just one thing...'

Mollie stopped and slowly turned to face her.

'If you want it, we've still got a deal.'

'Yeah,' said Mollie. 'I thought we must have, or mum and dad would have had the police all over them by now. Don't make much difference. We're done here. See that smoke?' she pointed to the woods. 'Dad's burning the rubbish at the camp. He won't stay after all this. That cottage will be back on the market. I'll be getting a new school.' She put on a rueful smile. 'Maybe we'll give Bristol a try.'

As Mollie turned away, to trot off down the hill, Gwynedd thought she heard her utter two more words. They sounded like 'thanks, anyway'.

They watched her move slowly all the way down the hill to the cottage, and then followed.

'She was the one that came to the cottage that night,' said Gwynedd. 'When you left the door open, and I moved the stone from the stream.'

'How do you know?'

'I just do. She was looking for you. Maybe she just wanted to get in the way, cause trouble, have a row, but lost her nerve. Maybe it was something else.'

'What was that about a deal?'

Now should have been the time to tell him about Len not being Mollie's real dad, but she realised that she didn't really want to. 'I'll tell you one day,' she said. Then she decided she had to tell him one small secret, to revoke one small lie.

'Last night, on the mountain, I didn't have my

254

mobile. Len took it from me, when I went to the camp.'

He looked at her and frowned. 'It was all a lie, then, about trying to phone and getting no signal?'

'The bit about there being no signal wasn't a lie, not a real lie. I mean, I dunno whether there's a signal up there or not. I bet there isn't.'

Sam shook his head. 'I won't ask why you do these things,' he said. 'But thanks for telling me. Now I know there's no point in phoning your mobile.'

They made their way back to town through the playground and the empty campsite. They stopped and looked at the rock. It had been there for millions of years, tough and unchanging. For a tiny part of its existence, they had borrowed it. Now they were giving up all claim to it. Gwynedd knew that she would never sit on it again. She made a mental note to take another route to the car park on Monday, when she went to catch the school bus.

There seemed to be an unspoken agreement that this was where they would say goodbye. They hugged each other, and she gave him a snatched and clumsy kiss on his cheek, just as he was beginning to pull out of the hug and let go of her. He looked as though he, too, was on the verge of tears.

'See you,' he said, and set off across the park.

'Yeah,' she said, not moving.

When he had gone a few paces, she called out to him. 'I'll save up and get another mobile.'

He halted and turned back. 'We get home from

Nan's on Boxing Day... or the day after. There's usually at least a week of the holidays left. You could come to Bristol then. Text me your new mobile number. As soon as you get it. Right?' He waved, and began to run up the path towards the town centre.

She was alone, but not quite alone. There was a little voice inside her that for some weird reason wanted to look on the bright side. There now, girl, it said. You got something to look forward to, and not just getting Dave's tea.